SURVIVAL

BLIZZARD

ESTES PARK, COLORADO, 1886

K. DUEY AND K. A. BALE

ALADDIN PAPERBACKS

FOR THE WOMEN WHO TAUGHT US THE MEANING OF COURAGE:

ERMA L. KOSANOVICH
KATHERINE B. BALE
MARY E. PEERY

———————————

First Aladdin Paperbacks edition March 1998

Aladdin Paperbacks
An imprint of Simon & Schuster
Children's Publishing Division
1230 Avenue of the Americas
New York, NY 10020

Library of Congress Cataloging-in-Publication Data
Duey, Kathleen
Blizzard / Kathleen Duey and Karen A. Bale. — 1st Aladdin Paperbacks ed.
    p.   cm. — (Survival! ; bk. 3)
Summary: When twelve-year-old Maggie attempts to rescue Hadyn during a sudden blizzard in the Colorado mountains in 1886, both cousins change their minds about each other.
ISBN 0-689-81309-0
[1. Survival—Fiction. 2. Blizzards—Fiction. 3. Cousins—Fiction.]
I. Bale, Karen L. II. Title. III. Series: Duey, Kathleen. Survival! ; bk. 3.
PZ7.D8694Bl 1998
[Fic]—dc21   97-3172
CIP   AC

CHAPTER ONE

"I hate Hadyn Sinclair!"

Maggie listened to the echo that came back across the meadow. There was patchy snow beneath her feet. Overhead, the dawn-gray sky was free of storm clouds—for the moment at least. Her father always said March weather in the Rockies was as unpredictable as a temperamental mule.

Rusty nosed at Maggie's shoulder and she shook her head, wondering if the tall red mule could read her mind. "Papa never meant you," she told Rusty without turning. Then she shouted again.

"I *hate* Hadyn Sinclair," the echo announced a second time in its hollow, reedy voice.

Maggie faced Rusty. "Mother says Hadyn

will be here four months, maybe five. His boarding school suspended him until next term. Uncle Thomas and Aunt Olivia must think it's good for him to spend time with us."

Rusty nuzzled her old blue coat. "What? What do you want? This?" She fished in her pocket for the last piece of carrot. "How am I going to stand Hadyn that long?" she asked as Rusty's soft muzzle brushed the palm of her hand. He crunched the carrot appreciatively, closing his eyes. Maggie checked the cinches on the pack saddle, then led him forward again.

Maggie followed the trail around the enormous snow-covered boulder everyone called Indian Rock. It was shaped like a giant man sitting cross-legged, bent forward at the waist. The wind had dropped, but it was still cold. In the distance, Maggie saw the Simms' ranch. They had built four new little visitors' cabins. There was smoke coming from the main house chimney. Maybe they would be coming to Cleave's store, too, today. She hoped so. They were good neighbors and nice people.

Maggie waded through a patch of deep

snow, the new, clean fall from last night dusted over an old, sand-spattered drift. She heard a telltale scraping sound and paused. Down by the Fall River, a bull elk was rubbing his antlers against a rough-barked pine. The wispy breeze was moving toward her. The elk had not caught her scent. Suddenly, he looked up and saw her. In two bounding strides the elk disappeared into a stand of aspen trees.

For a second, Maggie just stood still. There were so few elk left now, she almost never saw one. Her father said that it was the tourists as much as the hunters. With people roaming the mountains all summer long, the bighorn sheep, bears, and deer were thinning out too.

The sun rose warm and bright. It was a fine day and Rusty moved along at a good pace. The road was rutted, but not too badly—it would get worse after spring thaw. It was almost warm, and Maggie enjoyed the long walk. She spotted two deer and thought she saw some bighorn sheep on an outcropping high above the road. Before she could be sure, they disappeared into the craggy rock. She squinted, shading her eyes against the glare, but couldn't spot them again.

Crossing Black Canon Creek, Maggie let Rusty drink. Ice still laced the slow water along the banks. In the distance, Ypsilon Peak and Mummy Mountain were covered in snow.

Maggie patted Rusty's shaggy neck as they started forward. "I sure wish I didn't have to pick up the supplies today. Seeing Hadyn will be bad enough, but dealing with Mr. McAllister, too . . ."

Mr. McAllister loved to complain. Maggie was going to have to hear about every little thing that had gone wrong on the trip to the grocery store down in Lyons. Then on the way home, Hadyn would probably describe every muddy turn on the road. Maggie topped the last rise, and she could see Mr. Cleave's place. He lived in the little building that served as store and post office. His wife and children lived in the house across the muddy road.

"The Cleaves aren't arguing today, Rusty. At least, I don't hear them yet." She let Rusty set the pace down the snowy path. As they angled toward the buildings, she talked to Rusty over her shoulder. "Papa said last night we'll have a real town someday because so many Easterners are summering here."

McAllister's team of dark bays was tethered at Cleave's hitching rail. Up the Lyons road, Maggie saw a rig she didn't recognize heading west. Maybe someone from the Elkhorn Lodge was driving a rented turnout.

As she passed into the blue shadows beneath some tall pines, Maggie saw distinct mountain lion tracks in the new snow. She shivered beneath the thick wool of her coat. They had been hearing the big cats at night, and her father had found tracks by the pond.

". . . tell your mother she can't have more butter," Maggie heard Mr. Cleave shouting in his thick English accent as she got closer to the store. His children giggled as they ran out the door and back across the road to their house. A second later, Mr. McAllister came out.

"About time. I've been here near two hours."

"My father thought this would be plenty early. I'm sorry you had to wait, Mr. McAllister."

Frowning, Mr. McAllister crossed to his wagon. He untied the canvas cover and rolled it back. Without speaking, he hefted a fifty-pound sack of flour onto Rusty's pack saddle. Rusty grunted at the weight, his ears lowering, but he stood steady.

"Road was as bad as I've seen this year." Mr. McAllister turned back to the wagon. He moved several bags aside, then pulled one free. "Got you a hundred pounds of red beans. Storekeep in Lyons didn't have black beans."

Maggie kept her face entirely blank so when he looked over at her, there would be nothing in her expression to set him off. He shook his head and started talking anyway.

"I don't mind being the one to go down to the valley, but folks are just going to have to realize I can't always get what they want. I got blue calico for Mrs. Simms and I know she is going to pitch a fit when she gets here. Wanted red."

Maggie made a noncommittal sound and patted Rusty's neck as Mr. McAllister settled the bag of beans onto the pack saddle. Rusty grunted again. Maggie wanted to tell him that there was no use trying to compete with Mr. McAllister in the complaint department.

"Slid near sideways on that last downgrade going in. Mud's frozen now, but if it had been a warmer day, we'd have sunk farther. Good thing the nights have been cold. Took some fancy driving, I'll tell you that much."

"We sure appreciate it, Mr. McAllister," Maggie said politely.

"Thought we weren't going to make that last curve, either. That right side wheel just missed going off the track. Would have been the death of me and the team."

Maggie fought to keep from smiling. "Papa said to be sure to tell you that he was grateful, Mr. McAllister."

"I was watching that rear wheel so close I dang near got my eye put out on an old stubbed-off branch hanging low over the road. Saw it a split second before . . ." Mr. McAllister trailed off, pointing at a red mark on his cheek. "You can just see how close it was, can't you?"

"I sure can." Maggie nodded somberly. "I

guess I better go inside and ask after the mail."
Maggie sidled past him, then hurried away.

The door to the little store was ajar and
Maggie pushed it open. Mr. Cleave was sitting
beside his hearth. The fire was low and there
was a folded copy of the *Rocky Mountain News*
beside his chair. He was reading in the flickering firelight, his nose close to the page. He
looked up. "There you are, Maggie Rose. Come
warm yourself."

"Hello, Mr. Cleave," Maggie said as she came
through the doorway. "What are you reading?"

He held it up for her to see. *Bloomingdale's
Illustrated 1886 Catalog*, the cover read.

"They have everything from silk parasols to
eleven-dollar fine tweed suits. I'll send this
along for your mother when my wife has finished with it. It's more a ladies' book than anything else."

Maggie crossed the little room, pulling off
her gloves. She stood close to the fire.

"Has your father decided to give up on his
cattle yet? He was sounding pretty discouraged
last time I saw him."

Maggie turned to warm her backside. "He says we will keep them through summer, but I think he intends to build guest cabins like the Simms have—and sell off the cattle next fall. We're making more from summer boarders than ranching."

"You and all the rest. Old Lord Dunraven had that much right when he built the English Hotel. People are going to keep coming."

"I saw an elk on the way in. A big bull."

"Did you now? I heard Thomas Wood saying he'd seen a few cow elk over around Bierstadt Lake. It'll be a miracle if they ever come back. Dunraven's friends and the meat market down in Denver did their best to kill them out."

"Papa says it was pure stupidity."

"That it was, ruining the game herds in a paradise like this. And Whyte is still leading hunting parties from the English Hotel."

Maggie shook her head. "All any of our guests ever want to do is follow my father and me up mountains, sigh over meadows full of wildflowers, ride our horses into the ground— or picnic. Some of those men eat more fried chicken at one sitting than you can fathom."

Mr. Cleave laughed, then got up, laying the catalog on the rough plank table. He winked. "This is the day your cousin arrives, isn't it?"

Maggie nodded.

"It'll be good for you to have another young person up there, won't it?"

Maggie shook her head. "Not Hadyn."

Mr. Cleave laughed again. "How old is he now? I remember him as somewhat difficult."

"He's almost thirteen—a year older than I am—but he acts like he's five."

Mr. McAllister leaned in the doorway.

"It's a bitter day, I'm going home. Tell your father that we can settle up later. If you see the Simmses, say I'll bring them their goods in a few days. Give my regards to your mother."

"I will," Maggie said, bidding him good-bye. She pulled up the chair that Mr. Cleave used for visitors. Hadyn would arrive soon, and there was nothing she could do about it.

CHAPTER TWO

Outside the train window, the endless dreary countryside streamed past. In the light of dawn, the open land stretched to the horizon, broken only by the Rocky Mountains in the west. Hadyn felt sorry for the people who had to live here. He already missed Lafayette Square. It was the finest section of St. Louis. There were grand mansions, parks, and wide streets.

Hadyn winced, remembering his last visit to the primitive cabin his uncle had built. The smelly coal oil lamps made his eyes sting. It was almost impossible to read after dark. It was hard to do anything after dark besides listen to the wind or the wolves. Or his cousin Maggie. She could talk for hours about every tree, every kind of flower, everything that grew or crawled or flew. It made him tired just to think about her.

In St. Louis he and his friends often sneaked out of school to roam the streets, buying treats from the bakeries. Or sometimes they would go to a Speck's Confectionery and drink strong cups of Speck's superior coffee. They would sit, laughing and talking, until they had to go back. That was what had gotten him suspended. Coming back over the fence, he had run into the headmaster.

The train slowed. The conductor walked down the aisle. "Lyons Station. Please make sure you take all your baggage as you leave the train."

Hadyn peered out the window. The drab little town had grown since he had last been here, but it hadn't changed. The buildings were wooden, rectangles and squares—there was nothing anyone would call architecture here.

Hadyn stood up. His bag was on the luggage shelf. He slid it down, fitting the strap over his shoulder. Stepping from the train, Hadyn looked around. His father had assured him that it wouldn't be difficult to hire a wagoner to drive him the rest of the way.

Hadyn hitched his bag higher on his shoulder and started down the street. He had to ask directions twice, but finally found a livery stable off an alleyway near the outskirts of town. A circle of men sat around an overturned crate, playing cards.

"I'm looking for a driver to take me up into Estes Park."

A tall man with piercing blue eyes stood up. "I can take you, but you're about two months early for the summer season, aren't you?"

"I'm going to visit my uncle," Hadyn said tersely. One of the things he hated about the West was people's interest in other people's business.

"I'm Jeffrey Cole," the man said, extending his hand. Hadyn shook it, then stepped back toward the door.

Mr. Cole left his card game, to the complaints of his friends. "A job is a job, boys, especially this time of year. Besides, I have to earn back what I've lost here." They all laughed as one of them shuffled, then began dealing a new hand.

Hadyn stood uneasily, leaning against a stall as Mr. Cole harnessed his team and climbed up onto the driver's bench. Then the boy threw his bag in the back of the wagon and got up beside him.

"Now, this is not like taking a buggy ride through the park on Sunday," Mr. Cole said as he worked the team around in a tight turn and started down the alleyway.

"I've been here before," Hadyn said.

"When?"

"About two years ago."

"That's not what I'm asking. When did you come? Summer?"

"It was June tenth," Hadyn told him, puzzled. The wheel on Hadyn's side of the wagon dropped into a pothole. The jarring startled him and he grabbed the edge of the bench.

"June tenth is summer," Mr. Cole said, guiding the team around a frozen puddle. "If you've only been up this road in the summer, then you have no idea what it is going to be like today."

Hadyn didn't respond. This was another thing he remembered hating about Colorado. Everyone who lived in these little towns was so eager to impress any visitor with how rough their country was. Outhouses and bad roads seemed like stupid things to be proud of.

Mr. Cole slapped the reins over the horses' backs, and they rose into a reluctant trot on the muddy, uneven road. He didn't speak again until they were on the long, steep slope that led out of town. "It's better today than it has been. We got a cold spell in here starting three days ago. Before that the mud was deep. Now it's frozen again." Just as he finished speaking, the wagon hit a rut and jolted.

Hadyn tightened his grip on the edge of the driver's bench and nodded, hoping the man would keep talking. Anything was better than thinking about how much he wanted to go home.

"There's nothing a horse hates more than deep mud." Mr. Cole shook the reins. "Unless it's wading belly-deep in snowdrifts. I had a team once that plunged into a deep drift, then stopped dead. Not even the whip could convince them that the only way out was to keep wading."

"What happened?" Hadyn asked, feeling every bump in the road through the hard driver's bench.

"Got dark. All six of those horses froze solid that night."

Hadyn looked at the man's profile. There was no trace of a smile, or any other sign that he was joking. "Really?"

Mr. Cole turned to face him. "We broke them up with hammers and ice picks and brought them back down to the livery." Hadyn stared, then shook his head. Mr. Cole burst out laughing. "You aren't near as easy as most," he assured Hadyn. "Some of the Easterners believe every word I say, no matter how big a lie I make up."

Hadyn didn't say anything. He kept his eyes on the road ahead. Mr. Cole chuckled to himself, then fell silent, too. At the top of the rise, the road made a sharp, hairpin turn. The wagon swayed so close to the edge that Hadyn held his breath.

Mr. Cole was intent on his driving. The road rose steadily upward and Hadyn sat rigidly still. Two summers before, he had ridden in a canvas-topped wagon sandwiched in between six adult travelers. He had been able to see breathtaking glimpses of the mountains and the sky from beneath the wagon cover—but this was different.

Hadyn swallowed and looked down the steep drop on his side of the wagon. If the horses shied, if the wagon tilted and went over, they would tumble a thousand feet to the creek at the bottom of the slope.

"Do me a favor, son?"

Hadyn glanced at Mr. Cole. "What?"

"It's easy enough. I need you to sit over that rear axle, will you? A little weight can help keep us from skidding."

Hadyn looked into Mr. Cole's face for a long moment.

"Go on back, son. I wouldn't joke about a thing like this. I usually load a bag or two of sand, but I forgot."

Hadyn stood up and swung one leg over the

driver's bench, straddling it awkwardly for a few seconds before he managed to bring his other foot over. He hesitated, then took two more steps, bent over in a half crouch. The wagon heaved, jerking over a rut as he sat down.

Mr. Cole grinned at him. "Thank you, son. Just holler if you need anything."

Hadyn nodded, then looked aside so that Mr. Cole would watch the road in front of them. It was getting steeper and steeper. The horses slowed, blowing out great clouds of steam as they labored upward. At the next hairpin turn, Hadyn nearly cried out. The road switchbacked so tightly he was sure the wagon couldn't make it.

"Have to maneuver on this one," Mr. Cole said, and pulled the horses to a stop.

Hadyn stared out over the wagon gate as the team began to back up. At first, Hadyn was amazed to see how far above the town they had come. Then, as the wagon angled to the side and he could see down into the valley floor so far below, he was uneasy. Inch by inch the wagon kept creaking backward, rolling from one deep rut into another, then lurching free. The edge of the road seemed to disappear beneath the wagon, leaving nothing but air between Hadyn and a killing fall.

Hadyn took in a quick breath. "Mr. Cole?"

"Yes, son? You need something?"

"Can't you see how close we are to the—"

"Speak up, son," Mr. Cole said over his shoulder. "I can't quite hear you."

"Stop!" Hadyn nearly screamed. He stared, transfixed, at the curve of the stream far, far below. The wagon bed was slanted and the drop seemed to pull him toward it.

"The wagon hasn't moved for a full minute, son," Mr. Cole said quietly, and Hadyn heard him chuckle.

"That's why you really wanted me back here, isn't it?" Hadyn demanded. "To scare the pants off me?"

Mr. Cole turned around. "Now, why would I want to play a trick on a nice, mannerly boy like yourself?"

Hadyn stood up and walked to the front of the wagon, fighting the sickening pull of the precipice behind him. He clambered over the driver's bench and sat down, facing front. His stomach subsided and he felt himself beginning to calm down.

"Ready, son?"

Hadyn nodded, refusing to look at or speak to Mr. Cole.

"I charge double if you can't take a joke."

Hadyn kept his eyes fixed on the road, ignoring Mr. Cole's muffled laughter.

"Don't you worry. I'll have you to Cleave's before you know it."

"Take your time," Hadyn said. "I'm in no hurry."

CHAPTER THREE

Maggie sat at the kitchen table. She rolled her eyes as she listened to Hadyn describe his wagon ride up the mountain one more time. He seemed to think he was the first one ever to brave the Lyons road. And his story kept changing. The day before, walking back to the ranch from Cleave's store, Hadyn had sounded scared and angry. At dinner last night, nothing had bothered him much. Now, as they sat eating breakfast, he was laughing about how the wagon had almost gone off the edge.

"Maggie, finish your plate," her mother said.

"And a fine meal it is, too, Aunt Fiona," Hadyn said, smiling.

Maggie tried to keep the look of disgust off her face. Hadyn had been polite and complimentary to her parents—in other words, completely insincere—since he'd arrived. And both her mother and father seemed to be taken in by his act. How could they not see what he was really like? He had complained about having to sleep on the cot in the storeroom, groused about using the outhouse, and whined about carrying in firewood. He was worse than the finicky New York debutante who had come with her parents the summer before. At least she had *tried* to enjoy herself.

Maggie glanced at her father. He was folding his napkin, scraping back his chair. "I think I'll ride the north pasture and check the cattle. I want to break the ice on the creek up there if it's frozen over."

"Can I go, Papa?" Maggie asked, crossing her fingers beneath the table.

Her father shook his head. "Hadyn just got here yesterday. Surely you want to stay and visit with him."

Maggie made a face, and her father frowned.

It was a fierce look and she knew it well. She immediately smoothed her own expression. "I just thought you might need help."

"Your mother might, since you are kind enough to offer." He leaned close to whisper in her ear. "And you might change out of those old work trousers into your blue wrapper. Young ladies wear dresses." He kissed her nose, then got his jacket off the coatrack and jammed his hat down firmly over his ears. He winked as he closed the door shut behind himself.

Maggie's mother smiled. "There are walnuts to crack. Perhaps you two can do that while you talk."

Maggie averted her eyes as she got up quickly to help clear the table. Hadyn waited, his chair pushed back, an expression of pleasant patience on his face.

Maggie's mother bustled back and forth, bringing out a basket of nuts once the table was clean. "Here are hammers and the nutpicks," she said, laying them down. "Keep the mess off the floor, you two." She set out an empty basket for the shells and a clean bowl for the nutmeats.

Maggie sat down opposite Hadyn. She picked up one of the hammers. It was small, the perfect size for nut cracking; her grandmother had given it to her mother years before. Without looking at Hadyn, she went to work. She broke open five walnuts, then set down the hammer and reached for the slender steel pick.

"We have servants to do this at home."

Maggie flashed Hadyn a false smile. "You should have stayed there, then." She pried a walnut-half free of its shell and dropped it into the bowl.

After a long time, Hadyn began cracking walnuts, too. To avoid looking at him, Maggie glanced out the windows every time she raised her eyes. Twice, the sun dimmed as clouds chased across the sky.

Maggie's mother finished up in the kitchen and came back out. She settled into a chair by the fire and opened her sewing basket, then pulled out the tablecloth she had been working on since Christmas. It was cream-colored linen. The intricate embroidery was all in gray, vines and leaves bordering the edge. Maggie got up to stoke the fire so her mother wouldn't have to. When she came back, Hadyn was chewing. She glared at him, but he ignored her.

"Fiona!"

Maggie's whole body reacted to her father's anguished shout. She jumped up from her chair, breathless and afraid. Her mother was already at the door, flinging it open, the linen tablecloth on the floor where she had dropped it.

"Joseph! Oh, God!"

Maggie followed her mother onto the porch. Her heart froze when she saw the blood on her father's shirt, the unnatural angle of his right arm.

"It's bad, Fiona." Maggie heard the pain in her father's voice. Her mother whirled around.

"Maggie, hitch up the team. Hadyn, help her."

Maggie stood for a second, watching her father as he struggled up the steps, hunched over his bleeding arm.

"Maggie!" her mother snapped. "There'll be

barely enough daylight to get down to Lyons as it is! Hadyn, move along!"

Maggie ran toward the barn, hearing Hadyn's footsteps behind her. Her hands were trembling as she got the harness from its hook. "The two bays in the first stall," she shouted at her cousin. "Here!" She threw two lead ropes at him. "The one with the blaze will kick you if he gets the chance." She made sure Hadyn was headed in the right direction, then turned her attention back to the harness. By the time he led the horses out, she had everything laid out over the corral fence near the wagon.

Maggie harnessed the blazed gelding first. He was restless, and Hadyn had a hard time holding him still. The mare was easy. Once the team was hitched, Maggie got up onto the wooden bench, her knees shaking as she grabbed at the reins. Ignoring Hadyn's shouts as he jumped out of her way, she whipped the team into a trot and crossed the yard, hollering at the top of her lungs. The gelding reared as she jerked the horses to a halt.

Maggie's parents came out of the cabin. Her

mother put two blankets and an extra overcoat in the wagon, then ran back inside. Her father looked as pale as ivory as he struggled up onto the driver's bench. "Maggie. There's a cow with a new calf up there. Bring them down or that cat will smell the birth blood and get the baby tonight. And find my mare. She spooked after she threw me. Be careful."

"Don't worry, Papa."

Maggie's mother emerged carrying a covered basket. "I'll get word back to you. We'll be home as soon as we can." She hugged Maggie, then released her. "Hadyn, you listen to Maggie and help any way you can, you hear?"

Standing numbly on the porch, Maggie watched as the wagon rolled over the patchy snow, wincing when she saw it buck and jolt across the ruts at the end of the ranch road. She saw her mother reach out to steady her father, then the wagon rounded the corner and was gone, hidden by the pines.

"They're really going to just leave us here?"

Maggie turned to glare at Hadyn. "And what should they have done?" she demanded.

"We could have gone with them."

Maggie shook her head. "Don't you ever think about anything besides yourself?"

A wolf howled suddenly, somewhere off toward the northeast. Hadyn jerked around to face the sound.

"It's a wolf, Hadyn. At least two or three miles away. We haven't seen one all winter. If you want to worry about something, worry about mountain lions. We've had one coming onto the ranch for chickens and winter calves." Maggie felt the quaver in her voice. She was still shaking, but now it felt like anger.

"My parents will be furious when I tell them about this."

"If you want to go back down to the valley, then go. I don't need your help. In fact, you'll be in my way." Maggie stomped up the porch steps. She shut the door so hard that she heard a dish rattle in the kitchen.

Once inside, she stood in front of the hearth, automatically adding a log to the fire. She wanted to cry, but she couldn't. She looked blankly at the walnuts spread across the table, the half-full bowl, and the flecks of shell. Then, without meaning to, she pictured the blood on her father's shirt, the crimson lines running down his forearm to his fingertips.

Hadyn stood staring at the cabin door, his hands balled into fists. Maggie had no right to talk to him like this. And her parents were crazy to leave them here alone. He kicked at the icy dirt. The last thing he wanted to do was go back into the cabin.

He glanced toward the road. It would be easy enough to follow the fresh wagon tracks into Estes Park. Mr. Cleave would know someone who would drive him down to Lyons. And from there, he would just take the train back home. His parents would have to understand; after all, they'd never meant for him to be stranded in this wilderness.

Without allowing himself to think any further, Hadyn started walking toward the cabin. He could carry his bag, and he'd take some food. If he got thirsty, he could just melt some clean snow in his mouth. It was midmorning. He would have plenty of time to get to Cleave's before dark.

Hadyn jerked open the door. Maggie was standing in front of the fireplace, her gloves off, her fingers spread across the warmth.

"I'm going home," Hadyn said flatly. He walked into the little storeroom where he had slept the night before.

"What are you talking about?" Maggie asked from the other room.

"I'm talking about going home," Hadyn said evenly. "To St. Louis." He began gathering up his things.

"Hadyn. You can't go," Maggie said from the doorway. Her voice sounded tight, as if she were about to cry.

Hadyn looked up. "I can do whatever I want to do." He rolled up the last of his shirts and stuffed it in alongside the others. When he got home he would have the laundress wash and iron his clothes. Cook would have a meal ready within an hour of his arrival. He couldn't wait.

"You can't go home." The desperation in

Maggie's voice startled him—and made him angry.

"You can't stop me." He wound a scarf around his neck and jammed on his hat. Striding back in to the table, he scooped up the nuts they had shelled and put them in his pockets.

Maggie watched him, furious. "But my parents . . . and your parents—"

"Mine will be angry when I tell them about *this*," Hadyn said, gesturing at the empty cabin. "Anything could happen to us here, and your parents didn't give it a second thought."

"My father was *hurt*, Hadyn."

Hadyn straightened up, then slung his bag over his shoulder. "Do you want to come with me down to Mr. Cleave's store?"

Maggie shook her head, her eyes narrowed. "I have to stay here. Papa needs me to—"

"'Papa needs me,'" Hadyn repeated in a comically whiny voice. He knew she would turn red, and she did. "You ought to come with me, Maggie."

She stiffened. "I have to take care of the ranch. I'm staying."

Hadyn nodded. "You stay, then, but get out of my way."

Maggie stepped back and Hadyn crossed the parlor to the kitchen. He wrapped some corn bread and a hunk of cooked venison in a piece of newspaper. When he returned to the parlor, Maggie was gone. He went out the front door, closing it behind himself.

Halfway down the road, Hadyn heard Maggie shout at him. He turned and looked back at her, then went on. He was sick of people making him do things he didn't want to do.

CHAPTER FOUR

Maggie shouted at Hadyn until her throat hurt. She couldn't go chasing after him—she had to get the calf in. She stood, shifting her weight from one foot to the other, angry and scared. She could see Hadyn turning the corner, starting down the road.

Maggie bit at her lip. He'd probably come back in an hour or two when he got cold. She looked up at the sky. It was clouding up a little, the high wispy kind of clouds that sometimes meant a storm was coming. But even as slow as Hadyn walked, it would take only five or six hours to get to Cleave's store—and the weather would hold that long. Hadyn might even end up going down to the valley with her parents in the morning if anything delayed them and they had to stop overnight at Cleave's.

She squinted upward. The clouds were thin, so high she could barely see them. The weather would probably hold fair for days. She peered back out across the glaring snow. She could just see Hadyn through a gap in the trees. His shoulders were squared, his chin up. He looked like a little boy pretending to be a soldier. She shook her head. It had been silly of Aunt Olivia and Uncle Thomas to send him here. He hated it.

"And I hate him," Maggie said aloud. "He knows it isn't that dangerous to be here without my parents. He just wanted an excuse to leave." She watched Hadyn until the road curved and she could no longer see him, then shook her head and went back into the cabin.

Maggie banked the fire. She put on her coat and the hat her mother had knitted for her the winter before. Pulling on her gloves, she went out the door. She would take Rusty. He was calm enough to carry the calf. Her father's mare was pretty jumpy sometimes—and it might take a while to find her.

Rusty came out of his stall calmly and Maggie laid her face against the warmth of his neck for a moment. "We have to go get a calf and find Papa's mare, if we can." Rusty rubbed his jaw against her shoulder. "Hadyn left," Maggie said, feeling tears sting at her eyes. She straightened up.

Swiping at her eyes, Maggie got her saddle from the harness room. Rusty stood quietly as she bridled him, then tightened the cinch. She swung up and rode him out of the barn.

The north pasture enclosed the high ridge on the northern boundary of their land. To get to it, Maggie rode almost half an hour across the wide meadows that surrounded the cabin. As she went, she automatically scanned the horizon, following the fence line along the road when she could see it through the pines, checking for snow damage.

"If we're lucky, nothing will go wrong before Papa comes back," Maggie said. Rusty snorted a spring gnat from his nose, and Maggie frowned as though he were arguing with her. "Don't say that. Papa is going to be fine. He just has to." Maggie nudged Rusty into a shambling trot.

Rusty dropped back into a walk when they came to the long hill that led to the north pasture gate. By the time they were inside and headed across the first meadow, she had him trotting again. She rode catercorner from the gate, heading toward the open ground on the far side. The wind scoured the snow there, exposing the grass. She hurried Rusty along.

The cow was easy to spot. She stood apart from the others, less than twenty feet from a patch of red-stained snow. The calf looked sturdy enough. As Maggie rode closer, she could see that it was nursing.

"Where is that fool mare?" Maggie wondered aloud. A second later, she spotted her father's horse. The mare was grazing near a crooked pine that grew in the lee of a big flat-topped rock. Maggie turned Rusty toward the mare. The nervous sorrel tossed her head as Maggie approached.

Talking softly, Maggie slid from Rusty's back

and walked toward her. The mare bolted. She galloped across the clearing, reins dragging the ground, then dropped back to a trot as she went into a stand of pine trees. Pulling her coat tighter around her shoulders, Maggie swung up onto Rusty and followed. This time, the mare let her get within twenty feet, then shied away again.

Maggie strained to hold her temper, to keep her voice calm and patient every time she dismounted and started toward her father's mare. Even so, it took more than an hour before the nervous animal stood still long enough for Maggie to reach out and take hold of her bridle.

Relieved, Maggie looped the mare's reins around her saddle horn and remounted. Rusty plodded back downhill toward the cow and her newborn calf. Maggie looked up at the wind-torn clouds. They were still thin. She shivered. It was cooling off. She wanted to be back at the ranch well before dark. Maybe Hadyn had come to his senses and would be waiting for her. She shook her head. He was going to be useless even if he was there.

Lifting the calf was hard, but after a few tries Maggie managed to get it across her saddle and swung up behind it. She held the frightened calf close, grateful for the warmth of its soft coat. It kept licking at her gloved hands and rolling its eyes upward to see her face.

"Tell your mama to cooperate and we'll be home quick," Maggie said. The calf wriggled and she tightened her grip. Her father's mare followed, prancing a little, as Rusty ambled along. The cow was hard to get going, but kept up a good pace once Maggie got her started.

Getting through the gate was difficult, but Maggie managed to keep the cow moving. The calf started to bawl halfway down the long slope. The cow stopped in her tracks, confused. Maggie took off her glove and let the calf suck on her thumb. It quieted, and the cow calmed down and moved forward again.

Back at the barn, Maggie put the cow and her baby in an empty stall, then unsaddled her father's mare. She gave Rusty a whole coffee can of oats. He had earned it.

"Tomorrow after chores, I think we'd better go down to Cleave's place to see if Mama and Papa got started off toward Lyons. And we'll see if Hadyn is still there," she added, scratching Rusty's ears for a moment.

Once all the stock had water and hay, Maggie closed up the chicken coop for the night, pitched hay into the corral, and broke the ice on the pigs' water trough. Then she started for the cabin.

The fire had died down. Maggie stirred the powdery white ashes, finding a few buried coals. She used the hearth rake to gather them into a little pile, then split some thin kindling to lay on top of them. Blowing on the embers, she had a fire going within minutes.

Maggie heated some stew from the night before and sat close to the fire to eat her supper. Then she listened to the wind rising outside the little cabin and thought about her parents. It was a long time before she was sleepy enough to stop worrying and go to bed.

★　　★　　★

When he left Maggie standing on the porch shouting after him, Hadyn was feeling wonderful. For a long time, he enjoyed striding along in the crisp, cool air. For the first half hour, the road slanted downhill and he kept up a good pace.

The road was so rutted that he began walking beside it to avoid the freezing mud. His boots were wet. He stopped to brush at them. The leather was going to stain, he just knew it. *That* wouldn't make his parents happy. The cobbler's shop where the boots had been made was one of the most expensive in St. Louis.

He slowed down as the road started upward. He was breathing hard. The air this high was thin, or at least that was what people said. He ate the walnuts as he walked, wishing he were already on the train home.

A shrill sound made Hadyn jerk upright. He looked at the dark pines that edged this section of the road. Wolves? But it hadn't been a wolf, he was almost sure. He started walking again, feeling the pulse in his throat, glancing behind himself every few seconds.

Hadyn tried to re-create the sound in his mind. It had startled him so badly that all he could recall was how loud and sudden it had been. Could it have been an Indian war cry? Maggie and some of her friends had told him last time that there were still Indians in Estes Park, but he had never believed them. The only Indians he had seen were on the bronze pennies in Cleave's cash box.

A rustling sound in the trees brought Hadyn swinging around. He stared into the dense branches, every muscle tense. Seconds ticked past and he tried to still even his breathing so he could hear. The forest was quiet now; not even the birds were singing. Hadyn frowned. What kind of an animal could have made a noise like that?

Mountain lion. The words rang in Hadyn's mind. Maggie had said something about a mountain lion that had been killing their chickens. Would a lion attack a person? Hadyn shivered. The pine trees were dark against the snowy ground. Beneath them, the blue-green shadows seemed to swirl like water as Hadyn stared, searching for whatever had made the terrible sound.

After a few moments, Hadyn began walking again, looking uneasily over his shoulder every few seconds. He hunched over, pulling his bag a little higher on his back, then looked again. There was nothing behind him. Nothing but the rutted road and the legion of shadowy pines.

Hadyn pulled in a deep breath and started downhill toward a creek that ran across the road. He managed to jump from rock to rock without getting his boots wet. He kept walking fast. The forest was quiet. Maybe he had imagined the sound. He hoped so.

As Hadyn topped the rise, a second tearing roar ended the silence. He stumbled, terrified, then spun in a circle and began running, following a slanting course across a snowy meadow. He pounded away from the sound, too scared to stop, too scared even to look back. The ground seemed to blur beneath his feet as he sprinted, his bag banging against his shoulder blades.

Hadyn kept running, dodging around jutting rocks near a stand of aspen trees. He finally risked a glance backward, but it was impossible to tell if the big cat was following. The dark trees could hide a dozen mountain lions.

The ground sloped downward suddenly. Hadyn stumbled, almost falling. He staggered on, managing to keep on his feet. As the ground leveled out, his bag slid off his shoulder and he had to slow enough to shove the strap back in place. A branch covered by a low drift of snow caught at his boot toe and he stumbled again, breathing hard. He dodged to one side, barely missing a rotting tree trunk that jabbed up out of the frozen ground.

Hadyn stopped, half turning to scan the trees closest to him. These were aspens, not pines. Their milky white trunks were belted with curved, ash-gray scars. They had no leaves now and their limbs and twigs made a hazy barrier that blurred as Hadyn peered into them.

Could a mountain lion climb an aspen tree? Hadyn tried to see into the gray tangle of twigs. His eyes slid from the trees to a slanting pathway of open ground that separated the aspens from the next stand of pines. He kept his eyes moving as he turned in a slow circle; then he whirled around when he heard the soft snapping of a branch behind him. Breathing hard, he stared into the aspens and was sure he saw something moving. Without meaning to, he began to run again.

Hadyn swerved to avoid a steep slope and made his way across a clearing, skirting the edge of a stand of tall, slim-trunked pine trees. He ran until his breathing was ragged and painful, then staggered to a stop. There seemed to be small, ominous sounds coming from every part of the forest around him. He faced one direction, then turned back, dragging in quick, shallow breaths.

After a moment, he realized he was hearing a soft breeze moving through the branches. He stood still, trying to catch his breath, his knees quivering. He let his bag slide to the ground, clasping the leather strap in one hand. Had it been the mountain lion following him through the trees? He wasn't sure. But if it had been, he had done the smartest thing he could by running.

Hadyn turned around, his eyes moving across the rocks, the trees. He realized, suddenly, that the sun was dimming. He glanced up and saw thin clouds spreading across the arc of the sky. He pulled his bag up onto his shoulder.

The day was going by. It was chillier now than it had been when he left Maggie. He would just angle back to the road, avoiding the place where the cat had been. If he hurried, he was pretty sure he could get to Cleave's store before dark. If Mr. Cleave wouldn't put him up for the night, he'd go to the Elkhorn; there'd be plenty of room now in the off-season. Either way, he wanted to be headed down to the Lyons train station first thing in the morning.

Hadyn frowned, still staring into the trees. Uncle Joseph and Aunt Fiona might be angry with him for leaving Maggie by herself, but it wasn't his fault. He had offered to let her come with him. Hadyn took a step, then another— and then he stopped. He looked around. The aspen trees, the rocks, the pines went on forever in every direction. He blinked. He had absolutely no idea which way to start walking.

The wind was rising. Hands shaking, Hadyn opened his bag and pulled out a heavy woolen shirt. He took off his coat and buttoned the shirt over the one he already wore. As he put his coat back on, he tried to calm down. He wasn't lost. Not really. He wasn't that far from the road.

He looked at the sky. The clouds were thickening.

He started off, following his tracks across the clean snow. But at the top of the next ridge, the snow thinned and the patches of bare ground made it hard, then impossible, to tell which way he had come. Squinting, Hadyn thought he could see the road through the next stand of trees. He veered toward it, but when he got there, he found only a small meadow lined with dark pines.

For hours, Hadyn kept walking, scanning the land in front of him for any sign of the road, a ranch house—anything but the endless carpet of white. The wind got stronger, lifting little sprays of snow, piercing his coat.

As darkness fell, Hadyn came upon a field of broken rock. He found a crevice that could shelter him from the worst of the wind and hunkered down into it. At first, he felt a little warmer, but then the chill of the night began to work its way through his clothes. He opened his bag and put on two more shirts, then pulled his coat back on. He used the rest of his clothing to make an uncomfortable nest between the jagged rocks. With chattering teeth he ate the rest of the walnuts, quieting his hunger enough to feel his exhaustion.

As Hadyn crouched, listening to the howl of wind, he shuddered with cold and fear. He could feel the nearby forest, darker than the night. The icy fingers of the wind scrabbled over the rocks, trying to find him.

CHAPTER FIVE

When Maggie woke, the sun was high in the morning sky. It took her a few seconds to figure out why her father had not wakened her as he always did— to recall why her heart felt hollow and strange. Once she remembered everything that had happened, she rose and hurried into her work clothes. Then she lit the coal oil lantern with a long wooden match, turning the wick down so it wouldn't smoke.

The cabin was ice cold. Maggie could see her breath as she pulled on her socks and shoes. She had banked the fire carefully the night before, but even so, there were only a few small coals still glowing beneath the ashes.

Shivering, she built up the fire again and stood next to it. She spread her hands close to the flames, trying to warm them, then turned to fight the chill that seeped through her clothes. Only after she had turned back and forth five or six times did she venture to the front door and look out.

The wind was blowing, but not too fiercely. Maggie could see snowflakes streaking toward the ground. She went back inside. She found some day-old biscuits in the cupboard and put one of them and some cold beans on a plate. Then she carried the coffeepot in to the hearth and set it close to the flames. She warmed herself again. When she got back from chores, the coffee would still be hot. She had no time for a pleasant breakfast now. She wolfed her biscuits and most of her beans, then pulled on her hat and coat.

Out in the barn, Maggie checked on the cow and calf. The calf was stronger now, standing sturdily as it nursed. Rusty poked his head over the stall gate to have his ears scratched. When Maggie came out of the barn, it had stopped snowing, but the sky was still gray as far as she could see.

The chickens were glad to get out of their dark, musty coop. Maggie scattered the corn and a few kitchen scraps for them. Two hens argued over the beans she hadn't finished. The pigs squealed and grunted their approval when she dumped the slop bucket into their feed trough. She broke the ice on their water again, using a long pole to shove the biggest chunks over the side so it would take a little longer to refreeze.

Once the barn chores were finished, Maggie saddled Rusty. She headed him toward the north pasture. He walked slowly, obviously resenting work on such a cold morning. The gate wire had frozen to the post and Maggie had to find a rock to hammer it free.

The cows had drifted during the night, but Maggie finally found most of them in the lee of a stand of dense Engelmann spruce, their shaggy backs humped against the wind. She rode Rusty in a wide circle around them. They looked all right. They would move up to high ground to graze later if the snow didn't get worse. If it did, she might have to drive them down to the house pasture where she could keep an eye on them.

Searching the far end of the pasture, Maggie finally came across the remaining cattle. They were bunched up in a narrow draw. Slapping her hat on her thigh and shouting, she managed to drive them up to open ground. Once they could hear and see the other cattle, they broke into a voluntary trot and Maggie let Rusty slow his pace. She waited until they had settled into the herd, then turned for home.

Riding back toward the cabin, Maggie kept her head down. The wind burned her cheeks and stung her eyes. An explosion of hoofbeats startled her and she looked up to see three deer bounding away from her. Rusty lifted his muzzle and brayed and she laughed at him.

"You are just jealous, Rusty," she said. "You'd give anything to be able to run like that." She patted his neck and kicked her heels against his sides. He eased into a slow trot.

Maggie stopped to knock some snow from the limbs of her mother's favorite cherry trees. Rusty waited impatiently until she remounted, then started off before she could even touch her heels to his sides. "You think you're going to get to go back into your stall, don't you?" Maggie teased him. "Well, you can't. We're going down to Cleave's to ask after Mama and Papa. I want to find out when they left for Lyons."

Rusty trotted happily up the path toward the barn. Passing the cabin, Maggie saw an odd patch of white on the door. As she got closer, she could tell it was a piece of her mother's writing paper. Tying Rusty to the porch rail, she went up the steps. It was a note from Mr. Cleave.

Maggie and Hadyn,
Maggie, your parents asked me to come in a day or two to see if you two were all right. The way the snow is coming, I thought I'd best come this morning instead. I see the chores have been done and assume you are both out seeing to the cattle now. Maggie, your parents left my place at sunup this morning. Will let you know if I get any news. You're a good girl, Maggie. Don't worry too much about your father. Hadyn, your aunt says to remind you

*to do your share. I'll be back end of the week
or before.*

John Cleave

Maggie pushed open the door and went inside. Where was Hadyn? Had he just walked right past Mr. Cleave's store and gone all the way to Lyons by himself? She shook her head. It was too far and he hated walking. Maggie bit at her lip. Maybe Hadyn hadn't made it to Cleave's store. Maybe he had gotten hurt or something. Maggie folded the note and shoved it into her pocket. Now, she would have to go looking for Hadyn, instead of seeing if Mr. Cleave had found out more about her parents.

Maggie's hands were almost numb and she stoked the fire to warm up. Once the pins-and-needles feeling in her hands had let up enough so she wouldn't be clumsy, Maggie got down her hiking knapsack. For a moment she wondered if she really needed to pack anything, but she knew that if her father were here, he would insist that she be prepared for an emergency.

Maggie whispered a prayer that her parents were safe in Lyons and that the doctor could help her father. Then she set to work.

She filled her canteen with dark, sweet coffee and wrapped up a piece of venison. She put four biscuits in a napkin, then put all the food in a clean flour sack. She got her extra trousers and two thick flannel shirts and pushed them all into the bottom of her knapsack. She put the food in on top, then found the waxed matchbox and filled it with wooden matches. Last of all, she packed the bone-handled pocketknife that had belonged to her grandfather.

For a second, she thought about carrying a blanket, too, but it seemed foolish to risk getting any of their bedding wet or dirty. She could hardly do wash in this weather. Then she thought about her father's bedroll. He kept it in the barn; she would tie it to her saddle before she left just in case. Maggie drew the knapsack's strings tight, then tied a slipknot to hold it closed.

Maggie glanced at the clock on the mantel. It had stopped at nine the night before. She had forgotten to wind it—that was something her father always did before he went to bed. Maggie put on her faded blue coat and went out again.

As Maggie turned Rusty down the rutted road, the snowflakes thinned a little. Riding as fast as she dared, she pushed Rusty into a trot where the snow wasn't deep and the ground wasn't rocky. She kept her eyes moving, aware of the forest on both sides of the road. At first she followed Hadyn's tracks, but she lost them where he had crisscrossed the road trying to find a way around a snowdrift.

It was hard to ride into the wind. The snow flurried, then stopped, then started again, but the wind was constant. Maggie hoped it wouldn't keep rising. Sometimes in the winter, they got winds strong enough to bend the pine trees like saplings.

The road was slick and rutted. Along the top of a ridge, where the snow was a shallow dusting on the frozen earth, she managed to canter for a few hundred yards before the drifts deepened again and she had to rein in.

When Rusty slowed, Maggie glanced upward. The sky was darkening. She prayed once more that her father was going to be all right. There were three doctors in Lyons. Surely one of them could help him.

Maggie rode on. She could hear wind sighing in the treetops. Rusty settled into a rambling walk, covering the rough rocky stretch of the road that led down to Black Canon Creek, then back up. Here, on the north-facing slope, the ground was completely covered with snow.

Maggie suddenly noticed an odd, uneven set of tracks setting off from the road at a sharp angle. She rode closer. They were boot tracks, about the right size. Hadyn?

Maggie slid out of her saddle and led Rusty to the prints in the snow. The wind was softening their edges; it wouldn't be long before they would be filled in completely. If she had waited another day to ride the road, she might never have seen them at all.

A perfect print, sheltered between two rocks, caught her eye. She could even see the pattern of the shoe nails, a half circle in the center of the heel. It was Hadyn. No one in Estes Park wore fancy boots like that. Maggie slapped the reins against her thigh. Why had Hadyn left the road?

She stared down into the pines, then led Rusty along the side of the road, trying to see where Hadyn had come back up the slope. After she had gone a few hundred yards, she began to feel uneasy. If he had just been answering a call of nature, he wouldn't have gone very far off the road. Snowflakes settled on her back and shoulders as she remounted and tried to figure out what to do.

The night passed so slowly that Hadyn wondered if it would ever be over. It had been a long time since he had last heard the terrifying scream of the mountain lion; still, he was afraid the cat might appear at any second, snarling and close.

Hadyn hunkered a little deeper into the crevice, his ankles grating on the rock. The wind had eased during the hours of darkness, but now it was snowing harder. He shivered, as he had done all night. His layers of clothing hadn't really kept the cold from seeping into his bones.

Hadyn longed to stand up straight, to stretch. His whole body ached from his cramped position. He could feel, deep in his knee joints, a dull pain that had been sharp at first. He flexed his fingers inside his gloves and tried to squeeze warmth back into his hands.

A birdcall made him open his eyes. Hadyn lifted his head. The sky was finally getting light. It was still snowing. Flakes fell on his numb cheeks. Hadyn lurched to his feet, reaching out to steady himself against the jutting rocks. His knees barely held him up. He gathered his loose clothing and managed to stuff it into his bag.

Hadyn turned his back to the wind and found himself facing a thick stand of pines that were closer than he had thought the night before. In the gray light of dawn, the trees looked nearly black, their needles sharp and threatening.

His knees knocking against each other, his steps unsteady, Hadyn made his way slowly out of the rocks. Then, just at the edge of the boulder field, he stumbled again and crashed sideways. He fell, trying to protect his face. He skinned one wrist so badly it bled, but he couldn't feel anything—his skin was too cold.

Hadyn staggered to his feet. He had to find the road. He had to get to Cleave's store. For a second he imagined a fire, a warm hearth, and a steaming cup of coffee. He had been stupid, and he knew it. But the truth was, if it hadn't been for the mountain lion, he would never have gotten lost. Maggie should have told him the lions follow people like that.

As Hadyn walked, his hands and feet tingled, the feeling coming back into them. He walked with the wind at his back, his collar flipped up to protect his neck. He stopped to readjust his hat and his scarf and to pull his coat closer around his shoulders, then bent to pick up his bag once more.

When he straightened, he saw a glimpse of movement in the trees on a steep slope above him. He waited, holding his breath, watching closely. There. It was a horse, he was pretty sure. He yelled out, dropping his bag to wave both arms over his head. He saw the sorrel color of the horse's coat flash between the ash-brown trunks again, then disappear. The rider hadn't heard him. For a second Hadyn stood still, his eyes stinging, his heart pounding in his ears. Then he scooped up his bag and started running.

Halfway up the slope, Hadyn dropped back to a walk, gasping in huge breaths of frigid air. He struggled through deep snow, his boot soles skidding across rocks he couldn't see. At the top, he stopped. Three sets of tracks caught his eye, and he started toward them.

There had been three horses, Hadyn decid-ed. And their riders had forced them uphill. He could see the marks their bellies made as they lunged through the drifts. Their hoofprints were buried deep in the snow, but the paths they had made helped Hadyn climb after them.

It was much easier walking behind the horses, and Hadyn settled into a steady stride. All he had to do was follow the tracks long enough and the riders would lead him to safety. They

had to have a ranch house or a cabin somewhere nearby. Once more, the image of a
crackling fire taunted Hadyn. He shook his
head to clear his thoughts and forced himself to
keep going.

The horses' tracks led him onward. He could
see where they had floundered through deep
drifts and shouldered the snow aside, heading
relentlessly uphill. Hadyn stopped only once, to
take out the corn bread he had brought. Then
he ate as he walked, the food reviving him.

At the top of one ridge, the snow suddenly
gave way to dark, uneven rock. Hadyn slowed,
uncertain what to do. The tracks were impossible to see here. He searched the trees ahead,
hoping for another glimpse of the sorrel horse,
a chance to shout at its rider. He could see
nothing. Hadyn glanced at the sky. The clouds
were thicker and darker now. Snowflakes bat-
tered at his face.

CHAPTER SIX

Maggie shifted in her saddle and squinted up at the sky. It was snowing harder now. If she left the road to look for Hadyn, she could end up in trouble too. But what else could she do? Even if the Cleaves, or the McAllisters, or the folks at the Elkhorn Lodge were willing to come immediately, it'd be late afternoon before they really got started—if the storm let them search at all. And Hadyn had already been out all night. . . .

Maggie pressed her heels into Rusty's sides. He grunted, startled at her sudden decision, reluctant to step off the road into the drifted snow. She leaned down close to his long, shaggy ears. "Rusty, you have to be good today. I am

about as scared as I have ever been in my life."
She rocked her weight forward, digging her
heels into his ribs. Slowly, Rusty gave in, lifting
his hooves high in distaste as the snow deepened.

Maggie was heading straight into the wind at
first. Rusty plodded along, ignoring her pleas to
go faster. He walked with his head low, his ears
pinned back. Maggie skirted a rocky area, then
found Hadyn's tracks on the far side and followed them again. Where Hadyn had waded
drifts, Maggie had to get off and lead Rusty
through. He balked at the icy touch of the
snow on his belly.

The storm was getting worse. Maggie
looked behind herself every few minutes.
Rusty's tracks were filling in. In an hour or two,
if it kept up, they would be covered completely. Over and over, Maggie looked up at the sky
to orient herself, then remembered that the sun
was hidden by the thick, snow-heavy clouds.

Maggie came to a rotten aspen snag that
looked like an old lightning strike. More than
half the trunk was blackened. Beside it, Hadyn's

tracks stopped, turned, then stopped again. Maggie rubbed her hands together, pressing hard. She kept at it long enough to feel a little warmth coming back into them. Then she tightened her collar and pulled her hat down over her ears. How far could Hadyn have gone? He was headed straight away from the road now.

Maggie remounted. The thick stand of aspens ended at the base of a steep slope. Hadyn's tracks veered off to the north. Even though the wind had softened them, blurring details, Maggie could tell he had been running all out, skidding. She shook her head, tucking her hands beneath her thighs to warm them.

"What was he so scared of?" Maggie wondered aloud.

She guided Rusty across the clearing and uphill again, following Hadyn's tracks. He had still been running, that much was easy to see. With almost every step he had slid backward a few inches, sometimes leaving knee and glove prints in the snow as he lost his footing.

Hadyn's tracks kept changing direction,

sometimes plowing through deep drifts, sometimes angling off and running in long curves.
The tracks finally swerved and headed straight
uphill. At the top, Maggie let Rusty stop.

Blinking into the wind that scraped over the
crest of the hill, Maggie saw an expanse of broken rock. Some of the boulders were huge.
Many were deeply fissured, with wedge-shaped
cracks disappearing beneath the snow.

Slowly, Maggie rode around the edge of the
field of rock, her eyes on the ground. She
hunched her shoulders against the wind. It was
getting colder. She tried to remember whether
Hadyn had dressed warmly before he left. Even
if he had, he must have spent a miserable night.

Finally, on the far side, she saw Hadyn's
tracks again. The wind had blurred them and
the snow had dusted out the nail patterns. Still,
Maggie thought they looked a little newer than
the ones she had followed up the hill. Maybe
Hadyn had holed up for the night in the rocks.
She hoped so. They would have sheltered him
from the wind at least.

Maggie stared at the jumble of tracks. Hadyn

had paced a few steps one way, then another. "He was probably trying to figure out which way to go," Maggie said to Rusty, who tossed his head and sidled, trying to turn back. Maggie tightened the reins. "Not until we find Hadyn, Rusty." She looked back down at the ground.

After four or five false starts, Hadyn had set out in a beeline. The tracks headed downwind, but up a slope so steep that Maggie couldn't imagine why he would have chosen to climb it at all, much less in weather like this. To make matters worse, the hill was covered with thick stands of Engelmann spruce and lodgepole pine.

Ignoring Rusty's grunts and resistance, Maggie rode on. The ground beneath the snow was rocky. Maggie dismounted and led Rusty. The farther they went, the more puzzled Maggie became. This was terrible terrain. There were places where Hadyn had fallen, sprawling over snow-buried logs. Rusty plodded solidly along behind her, and Maggie was glad she hadn't brought her father's mare.

At last they were free of the trees. Maggie

blinked snowflakes from her eyelashes and tried to see where the tracks led. For a minute, she couldn't make sense out of what she was seeing. There were three deep paths that went uphill from where she was standing.

She worked Rusty closer, then stood looking down, shaking her head in disbelief. The hoof-prints were cloven, like two fat half-moons facing each other. Cows. What were cows doing up this high? They had to be strays, looking for yellowed grass uncovered by the wind. One of them was considerably smaller than the others—maybe a fall calf that was still with its mother.

"But why is Hadyn following them?" Maggie wondered aloud. She looked up the slope, then back down through the aspens. She lifted her gaze to the horizon. Mummy Mountain and Ypsilon Peak were invisible today because of the storm—so she would have to find another way to mark her direction.

Maggie faced the wind. Coming down the road it had been on her left, out of the east as usual. Hadyn had walked in a mile-wide curve.

He was moving north now, toward the high country. Maggie pulled off her glove and got a biscuit from her knapsack. She ate, stamping her feet. Rusty nuzzled her arm, begging for a piece of her food, but she patted him instead. There was no way to know how long the food she had brought was going to have to last.

Setting off again, Maggie realized that Hadyn had walked in the broken snow left where one of the cows had passed. She did the same. It made traveling easier on her, and on Rusty. The wind was getting higher and it would only get worse farther upslope. Maggie stopped a moment and checked her cinch and the ties that held her father's bedroll to the back of her saddle. Maybe Hadyn would decide to start back down soon, or already had. She could only hope that he would realize that he was heading into even more danger.

The cow tracks took a sudden turn and Maggie stopped to examine them. As she straightened, the icy wind biting at her face, she saw another set off to one side. Curious, she led Rusty toward them. The ground was crisscrossed with fallen logs, almost impossible to climb over. Rusty balked, snorting, his eyes ringed in white. Maggie tied his reins to a stout log, then went to take a look.

In an instant, Maggie understood what Hadyn had been afraid of and why the cattle were running uphill in a snowstorm. The paw prints were soft-edged and huge. It was a mountain lion.

Maggie stared at the tracks. The wind whistled through the bare aspen branches behind her. As she looked back up the hill, she realized it was snowing much harder than it had been a few minutes before. She could see only a few hundred feet in any direction.

Hadyn blinked. His eyes ached with cold, but he couldn't stop peering through the driven snow. Whoever the riders had been, they seemed to be as lost as he was. At every rise he had been expecting to see a ranch house, or a cabin, or a camp. At the least, he had hoped the riders would lead him back to the road. But all they had done was to keep blundering upward, in what seemed like an almost random path, skirting rocks and slopes too steep to clamber up. Now, their tracks led through a copse of aspen trees growing within a maze of fallen logs and fire-blackened stumps.

Hadyn staggered out of the stand of aspens, then hesitated, blinking owlishly, trying to clear his vision. The stark, white snow seemed flat, without detail. He squeezed his eyes shut for a few seconds, then opened them again. Suddenly he glimpsed movement up ahead.

Hadyn's heart leapt with hope, then crashed when he saw cattle lumbering through the deep drifts across the meadow. They were spread out; two of them were nearly into the trees on the other side. His eyes frantically followed the trodden snow from where he stood all the way uphill to the lead cow. Suddenly he understood. There weren't any horses or riders—and there never had been.

He balled his numb hands into clumsy fists and fought panic. Cows? How could he have been so stupid? He shook his head in disgust.

Instead of finding help, he had only gotten himself more lost—and in more danger.

Hadyn let his bag slide from his shoulder to the ground. He rubbed his hands together, blowing warm air into one glove, then the other. He tried to think, to figure out what he should do next. It was snowing harder. Maybe he should go down the way he had come up. He might have a better chance at finding the road again.

Hadyn turned into the wind, pulling his hat low over his eyes. Two of the cows were at the top of the slope now, headed back into the trees. Whether the ground rose or fell from there, Hadyn couldn't tell. Everything past the edge of the meadow faded into the blur of the falling snow.

Hadyn glanced down at the hindmost cow. It was smaller than the other two, he realized. Much smaller. And it wasn't moving. It looked like it had lain down next to a rock. Was it resting? Hurt?

Hadyn blinked again. As he stared down the slope, the smaller cow seemed to shudder, jerking back and forth. For a moment Hadyn couldn't understand. When he did, his heart slammed against his ribs and he held his breath.

The rock wasn't a rock at all. It was the mountain lion, its muzzle red with blood. It had killed the youngest cow and was now eating its dinner. As Hadyn watched, the cow's carcass shuddered again as the lion ripped loose another mouthful of flesh.

Hadyn stood helplessly, afraid to move, afraid to attract the big cat's attention. Walking sideways up the hill, Hadyn bumped into a blackened aspen stump. He stood, pressed close to it, unable to take his eyes off the mountain lion.

The wind gusted and Hadyn could hear the branches of the aspens below him rattling against each other. The snow stung the side of his face and he ducked his chin down into his coat collar.

Suddenly, the mountain lion straightened and raised its reddened muzzle. Hadyn caught his breath. The cat lifted its head, then turned slightly to face Hadyn. The big animal seemed to look straight into his eyes. As cold as he was,

Hadyn felt a clammy sweat rise on the back of his neck and on his forehead.

Moving like tawny liquid up the snowy hill, the mountain lion took one step toward him, then another. Hadyn swallowed, gripping the aspen stump so hard that his fingers ached. Hesitating, the cat looked back at the cow's carcass, then came forward again.

Hadyn moved backward without meaning to, stumbling over a fallen log. Scrambling up, he saw the cat breaking into a trot. His breath ragged with fear, Hadyn spun and ran.

CHAPTER SEVEN

Maggie was glad when the tracks turned out of the wind. The cows and Hadyn were all still headed upslope, so the going was rough. Nonetheless, it was a relief not to have the wind battering her face as she maneuvered Rusty through a stand of lodgepole pine.

Maggie leaned down and patted Rusty's neck. For a good hour she had been urging him along, making him go as fast as she dared. She wasn't sure what time it was, but it had to be well past noon. The storm would erase all evidence of the cows' passage by nightfall, she was sure. And Hadyn's tracks wouldn't last even that long. It was still snowing hard.

Rusty faltered, picking his way over a fallen log. Maggie reined in and dismounted again. This was a burn, the remains of a summer lightning fire. Beneath the snow, the ground was littered with blackened logs and half-burned branches. Riding over this kind of terrain was dangerous even in the summer. Maggie led Rusty more slowly up the steep, snow-slick grade.

As they emerged from a stand of aspen trees, Maggie searched the open ground ahead. The cows had strung out, the big calf falling behind. Maggie followed its trail with her eyes. When she saw the bloody snow she caught her breath.

Instantly, Maggie moved to Rusty's side, ready to mount. She scanned the tree line at the top of the slope, then turned and studied the grayish tree trunks below. Wind tears blurred her vision but she forced herself to keep looking. She half expected to see the mountain lion; it might be staying close to guard the calf's carcass.

Rusty was fidgeting. The wind was bringing him threads of cat scent, Maggie knew. He kept tossing his head, his nostrils flared and his eyes wide. Maggie talked to him softly, telling him that the cat had already eaten and it was probably afraid of people anyway. Still cajoling, Maggie tugged on Rusty's reins and got him moving, headed in the general direction of the dead calf.

It was hard going. There was loose rock beneath the snow and every step required concentration. Rusty was surefooted and steady, but this was asking a lot and Maggie knew it. She braced herself against the gusts of wind that buffeted her from behind. Squinting to keep the snow out of her eyes, she finally saw what she was looking for—Hadyn's tracks.

From the way the prints looked, Hadyn had seen the cat—or at least its kill. He had come this way following one of the older cows, then suddenly struck out at a sharp angle. Standing beside a blackened aspen stump, he had hesitated, then run. Maggie turned Rusty, following Hadyn's footprints in the snow; Rusty was happy to leave the strong smells of lion and blood. Hadyn had run across the mountainside, then veered, going straight upward again.

Maggie stopped, standing in Hadyn's boot tracks. She faced into the wind once more, staring at the trampled, red snow around the calf carcass. There. She could see another line of prints, this one carving a slender, graceful path through the deep drifts.

A sudden gust slapped at Maggie's face and she squinted. The cat's tracks led away from the calf, toward where she was standing now. Maybe the cat had gone after Hadyn? It wasn't likely, she knew, but it was possible if he had been foolish enough to try to scare it away from its kill.

Maggie walked slowly uphill, frozen rock rolling beneath her feet as she followed Hadyn's course up the mountainside. At the top of one ridge, the wind gusted, roaring past her. It knifed through a snowdrift, scattering it. She hunched, turning her face away, blinking at the tiny shards of ice. Struggling to keep her hat from blowing away, she pulled it down over her ears, then slapped her hands together until they tingled.

Rusty balked when she tried to go on. She leaned her weight into the reins, talking fast, promising him the biggest supper of oats he'd ever had if he would just move. Finally he took a reluctant step and she dragged him along, terrified that he would stop again.

With her eyes streaming from the vicious wind, it was hard to follow Hadyn's tracks. It was obvious that Hadyn was running scared. He changed direction often, sliding and stumbling, but always heading upward.

Maggie clenched her teeth, letting out an angry breath. Why was her cousin so everlasting stupid? The mountain lion had probably just been curious. It would never have followed him if he hadn't acted like a crippled deer, floundering and aimless. But even so, she reassured herself, it probably wouldn't attack him. Mountain lions rarely bothered people.

Maggie kept a constant pressure on Rusty's lead rope as she walked, wondering who was really the stupid one, Hadyn or herself? She raised her head and looked up the mountain. The burn extended as far as she could see. Even if she found Hadyn now, their chances were slim. She figured she could find her way back to the road eventually—but in a blizzard like this, she wasn't sure that would be fast enough.

Hadyn ran as hard as he could through the tangle of fallen logs. The air was so thin, it felt like it was pouring in and out of his lungs too quickly. His heart labored in his chest and he had to slow down long before he wanted to. He could still see the cat walking below him, its blood-darkened muzzle raised. It was following him, he was sure of it, toying with him the way a cat played with a mouse it was about to kill.

Hadyn tried to run again, but his legs felt leaden, his muscles numb. He stumbled, barely managing to right himself. Scrambling with both hands on the ground, he realized for the first time that he had left his bag behind. Fear as sharp as broken glass stabbed at him. He began to run again.

Forcing himself up the mountain, glancing back at the cat every few seconds, Hadyn tried to think clearly. He knew he had almost no chance of finding the road now. But maybe he should circle around and follow the cows again. They might be headed for some kind of shelter against the storm. Maybe, if he had stayed behind them, they would have led him to a barn, or even a ranch house.

Hadyn glanced back. The lion was a dim shape in the distance, but it was still watching him. He kept climbing, driven by his fear of the cat. The aspens closed in around him again, their trunks blackened, their bark scarred. Finally, after a long time, he was free of the aspen snags. He stopped, sobbing for breath.

He couldn't see the lion anymore. Where had it gone? Using one gloved hand to shield his eyes from the stinging wind, he tried to see back into the trees. If the cat was still following, it had hidden itself.

Hadyn faced the open ground above him. A sudden gust shoved at him, pushing him forward a few steps. Unable to stop glancing behind himself, he managed a heavy-footed, swerving run toward an outcropping of rock.

His whole body felt weighted by fatigue and hunger and fear. He forced himself to stagger on, grateful that the vicious wind was behind him.

As the wind got stronger, Hadyn could hear its shrieking through the trees below him and the boulders above. It punched at him, shoving him up the slope. Twice he barely managed to make his way past jagged rocks, pushing himself clear with stiff arms, cold, clumsy hands.

Hadyn could no longer feel the heaviness in his legs or the hammering of his heartbeat. With every step the wind pummeled him, forcing him along. He could see beyond the outcropping of rock now, and what he saw terrified him. It looked like the land dropped away. All he could see was the swirl of snow in empty space.

There were twisted, malformed trees among the rocks. Their tortured silhouettes were lopsided, as though the high winds had ground away half their branches. They bent in the gale and Hadyn caught hold of one, stopping himself for a few seconds before a gust of wind wrapped itself around him, breaking his numb-fingered hold.

Grabbing at every boulder, clawing to reach another tree, Hadyn inched closer to the out-cropping. Terrified, he realized that the margin between life and death was narrowing. If he could angle far enough to his right, the wind would shove him up against a solid wall of rock. If he couldn't, it would blow him over the edge.

Hadyn couldn't stop and the driving snow wouldn't let him see how far he would fall if he missed the rocks. It might be ten feet, or a thousand. The gale was a force, a howling presence that seemed to take away his strength, his breath, his will.

CHAPTER EIGHT

"Oh God, Rusty, you have to," Maggie pleaded, pulling on the reins. The last stretch of terrain had been awful. In the burn, every step had been treacherous. But now that they were almost to open ground, Rusty had balked.

Rusty stood solidly, his head lowered, his eyes closed against the wind. Ice clotted his eyelashes and the insides of his shaggy ears. He had stopped in front of a fallen log and refused to step over it. Maggie threw her weight against the reins, leaning to one side, trying to pull Rusty off balance, to force him to take a step. When he would not, she pretended to give up. The instant she saw him relax, Maggie heaved on the reins again.

To keep from falling, Rusty took a step toward her, then ambled a few paces forward. But he balked again and would go no farther. His ears were pinned back now and he shook his head, his eyes stubbornly on the ground. Maggie collapsed against his side. The gusts slammed at her, driving the cold through her coat, into her heart. Her hands were numb; her feet ached with cold. Still pressed close to Rusty for warmth, she put her back to the wind and looked up the mountainside.

She was closer to timberline than she had thought. In the distance, she could see krummholz trees, beaten into dense thickets, shaped by the constant winds. She had always admired their toughness, growing where almost nothing else could grow. Their trunks were always twisted and they rarely got taller than a man. It was so strange—her father said some of them were hundreds of years old.

Among the krummholz, a flicker of movement caught Maggie's eye. Against the unbroken white of the icy ground, and blurred by the curtain of driven snow, someone was running wildly, arms outflung, coattails flying. Maggie blinked, narrowing her eyes, trying to see more clearly. For another instant, the form was visible, then some trick of the wind, or the lay of the land, erased it and she could see only endless white again.

For a moment, Maggie could do no more than stand, staring. Then she managed to free her voice. "Hadyn!" she shouted, but the wind muted her cry and she knew that even if it was Hadyn, he would never be able to hear her at this distance.

She dragged at the reins, trying to make Rusty follow her. He raised his muzzle to ease the pressure on the bit in his mouth, but he would not move.

Maggie faced him, frantic, her eyes squeezed almost shut against the wind. She doubled the reins and lashed at his flanks, but he continued to stand still. Furious, she got behind him and shoved at his rump, slapping and berating him, then pleading again. None of it did any good— Rusty would not budge.

Shaking with urgency, glancing upslope, Maggie unsaddled Rusty, then tethered him to the fallen log. She could not leave him for long—not here where a cat or wolves could so easily find him. But she had to tie him; there was nothing else she could do. At least he would be free of the tight-cinched saddle for a while, and could rest.

Rusty raised his head and looked straight into her eyes. "I'll be back," she told him. The red mule nosed at her sleeve, obviously confused. She patted his forehead. "I'm sorry, Rusty, but I have to go after Hadyn."

Maggie bent to untie her father's bedroll from the back of the saddle. Hadyn could use it as a cape if he was chilled through. Or maybe they could sit down on it and eat something before they started back down. Her hands were clumsy with cold and she had to pull off her right glove to loosen the latigos. Then she untied her knapsack and slid it up over her shoulder. When she straightened, the wind ballooned her coat and she shuddered as the cold air worked its way through her heavy cotton shirt.

Maggie carried the saddle and saddle blanket to an aspen stump. She placed them as high off the ground as she could. Then she started walking. It was easier going uphill without Rusty. Still, Maggie went slowly, placing her feet carefully, leaning back against the impatient rush of the wind. She clutched the bedroll first under one arm, then the other. Finally, she stopped to tie it across the top of her knapsack. It hung awkwardly and flopped up and down, but at least her hands were free.

Turning, Maggie looked back toward Rusty. He had slipped his bridle and was picking his way carefully downhill. She caught her breath. He was far enough away that Maggie knew she would never catch him. Helpless to do anything else, Maggie watched him take tiny, mincing steps as he recrossed the burn. She said a little prayer for his safety, then one for her own—and Hadyn's. Then she started walking again.

As she climbed, Maggie frowned. Where did Hadyn think he was going? She lowered her head and trudged along, making the best speed she could. The higher she got, the more frightening the force of the wind became. Even the dwarfed krummholz trees seemed overwhelmed by it. They swept the snow, their deformed branches arcing wildly back and forth.

At the top of the ridge, Maggie paused. The gusts were nearly lifting her off her feet. The land sloped upward toward a series of rocky ledges on one side—but to her right, it looked as if there was nothing between the ridge she stood on and a clifflike drop-off.

As Maggie hesitated, the force of the wind escalated. She could barely stand. She squeezed her eyes shut, then forced them open again, trying to see where Hadyn had gone. She glanced toward the precipice. If he had gotten close just as a big gust came . . . . She shuddered and took a single step forward, angling to her left, toward the rocks.

Another blast of wind knocked Maggie down. Her knapsack slid awkwardly askew. Instinctively, she grabbed at a rock and held on as the wind somehow found its way beneath her body and lifted her for a second, like swift water lifting a swimmer. Unable to get to her feet in the violent gale, Maggie hung on through the gust, then relaxed her hold a little.

Another pounding surge blew her upward along the slope and she scrabbled for a hand-hold. Fear beating in her chest, Maggie waited for the wind to subside again. The instant it did, she leapt to her feet and sprinted toward the rocks, her knapsack and bedroll thumping against her back with every labored step. The next gust caught her within a few strides and knocked her flat.

On her belly, Maggie pressed against the earth, anchoring herself on a jutting rock. When the wind paused to take a breath, Maggie leapt up again. This time, she managed to position herself almost in line with the rock ledges before the next gust slammed her back down.

The gale held steady this time, surging around Maggie like a river. It lifted her again and she could only hang on, gripping jagged rocks with both hands. Her fingers were numb and her left hand began to slide on the snow-slick stone. Fighting to keep her hold, Maggie

cried out in terror as the force of the wind lifted her a little higher off the ground. An instant
later, her hand slipped free.

For a horrifying instant, Maggie was sure she
was going to be blown over the edge. Frantic,
aiming for the ledges, she clawed at the ground,
searching for a new handhold. Because her
body was no longer aligned with the wind, the
next gust caught the slight angle of her legs.

Helpless to do anything but scramble for
new grips on the frozen ground, Maggie felt
herself swinging in a barely controlled circle. As
her body reached the halfway point, the roaring
gale very nearly tore her loose from the
ground, but she managed to hang on. A few
seconds later, she felt the full force of the next
surge. She was still on her belly, but now she
was facing downslope, her feet leading the way
uphill.

Maggie could not keep her eyes open.
Wind-borne sand and tiny bits of ice cut into
her skin. She lifted her head, craning back over
her shoulder to try to see the outcroppings
above. She got only a second's glimpse, but it

was enough. She wasn't far off now. If she could follow a slanting path, she would be safe from the drop-off.

It was easier feet first. The wind still snaked its way beneath her and would have ripped her free if she hadn't held on strongly, but now she could use both her hands—and both her feet. Fighting the screaming gale, inching upward, opening her eyes only when she had to, Maggie got closer to the rocky outcropping.

Her mind focused on what she had to do, Maggie felt time slow down. There was nothing in her world beyond the rocks she gripped, then released, easing herself upward. The roar of the wind and the constant stinging pain of the sand and ice in her face seemed to have been there always. When her feet butted against the first of the low rock ledges, it took her a moment to understand that she had made it.

Crawling along the jagged ledges, Maggie finally found her way into a narrow fissure deep enough to shelter her. For a long time, she lay still, dragging in deep breaths of the freezing air. Then she managed to sit up. The screaming of the wind made her tremble. It was like a wild animal, angry that she had escaped it.

Maggie untied her father's bedroll and sat on it to protect herself from the chill of the rock. She slapped her hands together, trying to warm up. She flexed her toes and rubbed her legs. After a long time, she began to feel the painful tingling that meant life was coming back into her hands. A few minutes later, her feet began to warm up enough to ache.

Exhausted, and grateful beyond words to be out of the wind, Maggie opened her knapsack. She held the canteen in trembling hands and took big, greedy swallows of the sugary coffee. It was so cold that it hurt her teeth, but was delicious and she began to feel a little strength returning to her body—and a little hope.

Hurriedly, Maggie ate a biscuit and drank more coffee. Then she repacked her things and got cautiously to her feet, staying bent over far enough to remain out of the wind. The sky had darkened, but whether it was late afternoon or simply a false dusk created by thickening clouds, she wasn't sure. Following the fissure, Maggie made her way forward.

The rock ledges had formed a complex maze. Maggie turned to the left, then to the right, then back again. Just above her head the wind shrieked over the stone. It was still snowing, and in places there were little drifts among the rock.

Maggie straightened up where the fissure deepened. It reminded her of the long gash in Old Man Mountain behind the Elkhorn Lodge. Along one side, a half cave had formed, angling beneath the rock. Maggie blinked, trying to see into the shadows.

A dark shape made her stop midstride. Anything might have taken shelter here—a lion, a wolf . . . . But it wasn't. Almost weeping with relief, Maggie ran to Hadyn. An instant later, her relief froze back into fear. He wasn't conscious, and she wasn't sure he was breathing.

CHAPTER NINE

Hadyn was curled into a ball, like a child sleeping on a cold night. Maggie slid her knapsack off her shoulders. Fumbling with the ties on her father's bedroll, she crouched beside her cousin. Once she had the thick, quilted blankets unrolled, she spread them out.

Stooping, Maggie worked her hands beneath Hadyn's shoulders. It took her several tries, but she managed to get him onto the blankets. His scarf had come undone and Maggie rewrapped it, covering his head and neck. She chafed his cheeks and slapped him gently, but he did not respond.

Maggie pulled off Hadyn's boots and rubbed

his feet, hard. Once the skin looked pink again, she tucked the blanket around his legs and went to work on his hands. He took in a deep shuddering breath and she paused, waiting for him to open his eyes, but he didn't.

"Come on, Hadyn," Maggie whispered. "Come on. You have to be all right."

Maggie rocked back on her heels, reaching to pull the blankets up to Hadyn's chin. Working desperately, she rubbed his shoulders and chest through the quilts, then scooted around to work on his feet again. Switching back and forth, she kept trying to warm Hadyn, to rouse him. Twice she sipped a little of her sweet coffee, but she was conscious now that she should save most of it for Hadyn.

The roar of the wind had been so constant Maggie had stopped noticing it. Now it dropped a little and she looked up, startled. The sky was darkening. It was hard to tell through the thick clouds, but it looked like there was only an hour or so of daylight left.

"Oh, please God," Maggie whispered.

She stood up slowly, cautiously. The wind

was still strong, but nothing like it had been. She glanced upward again. As cold as it was now, it would be much worse before morning. They had to have a fire.

Maggie tucked the bedroll closely around Hadyn, then rummaged through her knapsack. The matches were safe in their waxed container and she set them carefully on the ground. She pulled out the flour sack that held the biscuits and venison. The smell of the meat made her mouth water, but she forced herself to put it down beside the matches. Hurrying, Maggie reached into the bottom of her knapsack and took out the two heavy cotton shirts and her spare pair of trousers.

Deciding quickly, Maggie kept out the two shirts and repacked everything else. She checked Hadyn once more, then stood up again. The wind caught at her coat and made her shudder as she clamped her arms against her sides, flattening the cloth close to her body.

As Maggie made her way down the fissure through the maze of low ledges, she stopped twice to build little cairns of stones to mark her way. Looking over the top, she spotted a clump of krummholz trees, the windward side brown and dead. She followed the last ledge and stepped cautiously into the open. The wind was still strong, but she kept her feet easily.

Going as fast as she could, Maggie doubled back, crossing the open ground, following the lowest rock ledge. She found the krummholz easily, but she hadn't seen the sharp incline above it.

She slewed sideways, digging her heels into the frozen soil, and sledded downward. Shielding her face with her arms, she skidded into the sharp-needled boughs and sprawled to a stop. As she sat up, Maggie noticed that the air was still. A boulder as big as the cabin she lived in sheltered the stunted pine thicket on one side, and drifted snow stopped the wind from the other.

Standing up, Maggie pulled her gloves off. She laid the two shirts out on the ground side by side. She took one blue sleeve and one red and tied them together. Then she stepped around the shirts and made her way beneath the dead, brown-needled part of the krummholz closest to the boulder.

Once she had crawled through the lowest of the branches, Maggie found she could stand up. The old twisted limbs had rooted wherever they touched the earth and formed a rounded canopy that made the krummholz look less like a tree and more like a lopsided thicket. Snow had nearly buried the downhill side, the drift forming a wall that had held against the worst winter winds. The lowest layer of snow was dirty gray—it had probably been there for several years.

Maggie set to work, half stooped as she made her way to the central trunk. Where the pine had died back, the smaller branches snapped off easily. Maggie backed her way out of the krummholz over and over, stacking armloads of splintered wood across her shirts. Every two or three trips she sat on the brittle brush, compressing it. Once she had enough kindling, she tried to get larger branches.

Because the wood was dried so completely by the constant freezing cold and the winds, it was light and fragile. Using only her hands, Maggie managed to break off branches as big as her wrist. Using a stone for a hammer, she got four or five bigger ones.

When the pile of brush and branches on her shirts was big enough, she pulled the outermost sleeves up and over, tying them together to form a tight circle of flannel around the middle of the stack of wood. Then, breathing hard, Maggie stepped back and glanced at the sky. If she hurried, she would have time for one more load.

Maggie rolled the bundle of wood forward so that the knot in the ends of her shirtsleeves was easy to reach. Using it as a handle, she hoisted the load of wood onto her back. She could manage the weight, but it would be difficult. She looked up the mountainside.

The sharp incline that she had skidded down so fast seemed five times as long now. Twice, Maggie started upward and fell back, unable to balance the weight of the wood. Feeling her stomach tighten, she sat panting to catch her breath. If she couldn't get the wood back up to Hadyn, they wouldn't make it through the night.

The wind whistled through the rocks above. Maggie shuddered, remembering her body lifting, being driven along against her will. If the wind came up again, she wasn't sure she could make herself brave the drop-off a second time. She balled her hands into fists, stamping her feet to warm them. She glanced at the rounded canopy of the krummholz and hesitated, an idea forming in her mind.

Dropping to her knees, Maggie squeezed back into the little sheltered room formed by the wind-tortured branches. Using a stout limb to gouge at the ground, she began to dig.

Hadyn felt a weight on his chest. He had no idea what it was or where it had come from. It was dark where he was now, and there was little sound, only a distant whining, like someone singing a vague, sad song.

Slowly, Hadyn became aware that he was uncomfortable. He rolled onto his side, drawing his knees up close to his chest. It was cold and still very dark. His bed seemed too lumpy, too hard. Was he dreaming? The whining sound seemed to get louder and he wondered what it was.

A trembling began in Hadyn's legs and passed upward through his body. It got worse, until he was shuddering, almost convulsing. He was cold, too cold. What was wrong? He had the awful thought that he might be dead. He wasn't sure why he thought it was likely, but somewhere deep in his heart, he knew it was. Frightened, Hadyn opened his eyes.

For an instant he was confused by what he was seeing. Some kind of dark, uneven wall rose crookedly over his head. Above it was an irregular strip of dusky light. The sky? The mournful whining went on and on, rising, then falling.

Hadyn blinked and uncurled his body, his teeth chattering uncontrollably. Sitting up slowly, he leaned forward, nauseated. He rubbed his hands together as parts of his memory came rushing back. He could recall the terrible wind and the cliff he had been so sure he was heading straight toward. He shook his head to clear his thoughts.

Fingering the bedroll, Hadyn tried to remember how he had gotten here. He could vaguely recall struggling toward the rocks in the howling wind. Obviously someone had helped him—someone who had the kindness to wrap him up in a bedroll. But where had he gone? Hadyn leaned out from beneath the overhanging rock, then ducked back. It was snowing.

Abruptly, Hadyn realized his bag was gone. Where was it? He frowned. Like puzzle pieces falling into place, images of himself leaving the ranch and Maggie yelling at him from the porch appeared. He recalled the mountain lion, too, and running away without his bag.

Hadyn clenched his teeth. How had he gotten here, and where had the person who'd helped him gone? He sat up straighter. His boots were set side by side near the rock wall, his gloves draped across them. Then he saw a knapsack lying a few feet away.

The wind was dropping, but now it was snowing harder. In the hush left behind by the slackening wind, Hadyn thought he heard someone coming. He struggled to his feet. The bedroll made him lurch to one side, but he managed to catch his balance before he fell against the rock. The footsteps were coming closer. Hadyn kicked free from the blankets, then turned to grab his boots. Maggie had told him about all the crazy miners who still lived up in the mountains. All he wanted was to get home. If some old man living in a shack would get him back to Lyons, he was sure his father would be willing to pay a reward.

Hadyn was trembling as he pulled on his boots. His fingers were numb, clumsy. The footsteps were getting closer. He reached down for his gloves.

Straightening up, Hadyn stood unsteadily. His scarf had come undone and he pulled it off, then rewrapped it around his neck, never taking his eyes off the curving rock ledge. He heard the dry rattle of stone against stone.

CHAPTER TEN

The wind was easing up, but it was snowing a little harder as Maggie made her way up the mountainside. There wasn't much daylight left. She wasn't sure how she was going to get Hadyn down to the krummholz tree, but she had to think of something. By leaving the firewood down below, she had eliminated any other choice.

The main thing was to hurry: Maggie knew that she had to get a fire started, and soon. She had to get Hadyn warmed up—and herself. As cold as it was now, it would get far colder by morning. And there was every chance that the wind would come back up.

She ran a few steps, then tripped, flailing

wildly with her arms to catch her balance. She forced herself to slow back to a walk. She was already exhausted. It would be stupid to fall now. If she got hurt, neither she nor Hadyn would ever get home.

The fissure seemed longer than it had before. Maggie was glad she had built the cairns to guide herself through the maze of rock ledges. Walking heavily, sometimes sliding on the loose rock, Maggie finally came around the last curve.

The bedroll was twisted in a heap. For a few terrifying seconds, Maggie thought the cat had found them. But then she noticed that Hadyn's boots were gone.

"Hadyn!" Maggie's cry rang on the rocks.

She was about to yell again when she saw him step into sight. He smiled weakly. He looked so awful she felt sorry for him—but she was still angry.

"Maggie." He came toward her.

She could see the fear in his eyes, and her anger faded. "I found a good place where we can build a fire and spend the night." She pulled the canteen out of her knapsack and handed it to him. "Can you walk?"

Hadyn took a long drink of the sweet coffee. Then he nodded. "I think so. How did you find me? I thought I was going to die out here." He sipped at the coffee.

Maggie shook her head. "You left a trail that a two-year-old could have followed."

"I saw some cows—"

"And a mountain lion," Maggie interrupted. She watched astonishment cross his face. "Mountain lions leave tracks too, Hadyn."

Hadyn shivered. "It came after me, Maggie. It could still be close."

"I expect he's still finishing supper," Maggie said, shaking out the bedroll. She rolled it up and handed it to Hadyn. Then she grabbed her knapsack and shrugged the straps over her shoulders. "Let's go."

Hadyn hesitated. "It's almost dark, Maggie. We should stay here."

She shook her head, too tired to argue. "No, Hadyn, we shouldn't. If the wind gets bad before morning, we could end up stuck in these rocks until it drops again. And besides, there's firewood down there."

"Firewood," Hadyn echoed.

Maggie nodded wearily. "Come on." She started down the fissure, glancing back three or four times to make sure he was following. Her legs felt like lead and her whole body ached. But she knew she still had work to do. She could only hope that Hadyn would be able to help her.

Maggie went slowly—she had no choice. It was getting hard to see. Hadyn managed to keep up most of the way. Maggie waited for him at the top of the incline above the krummholz, snow swirling around them.

"Down there?" Hadyn asked, coming to stand beside her.

Maggie nodded. "Can you make it?" She swayed on her feet, desperate to get going, to get a fire made.

Without answering, Hadyn started forward cautiously. Maggie waited until he was halfway down, then followed. He lost his footing and sat down hard, skidding the last dozen feet to the bottom. He came to rest a few feet from her bundle of firewood.

Maggie felt an absurd laugh rising in her throat. It was all she could do to keep from giggling as he stood up, brushing at his pants. She took the bedroll from him and dusted off the icy soil.

"Go under," Maggie instructed Hadyn.

"What?" he said, frowning at her.

"Under the branches. It's sheltered in there, almost like a snow cave."

Hadyn hesitated, so Maggie went past him, ducking beneath the twisted limbs. "Come on, Hadyn."

Maggie waited, bent over, until he had made his way into the still, dark shelter of the krummholz. Then she dragged the firewood bundle in after them. "Get the matches out," she ordered Hadyn, pushing the knapsack into his arms as he sat down.

While Hadyn fumbled through the pack, Maggie laid a fire in the pit she had dug, making sure there were no dry, overhanging branches. She used tiny twigs to start with, layering them closely. She wished for a little paper, or even dry moss, but that was impossible, she knew. Adding slightly bigger twigs to the pile, she turned and looked at Hadyn.

"Here," he said, holding out the little waxed box.

Maggie took the matches from him and struck one, cupping her hands around the flame. She lowered it to the dry tinder. The flame flickered and popped, growing.

"God," Hadyn breathed. "A fire."

Maggie didn't answer him, but she knew he wasn't swearing. It had been a prayer of thanks. The flame seemed like a miracle to her, too. It crackled, spreading slowly at first, then more quickly. Within a few minutes, they had a real campfire. Maggie sat so close to it that the soles of her shoes steamed and she could smell the wool of her coat. Still, she wanted to get closer. The orange firelight glowed on the branches above them.

"I really thought I was going to die, Maggie."

Maggie looked up. "You came close. We both

did. And we still have a long way to go."

The instant she saw the fear leap back into his eyes, Maggie was sorry she had said what she did. But it was true, and there was no point in babying him. Or herself.

"I'm sorry, Maggie," Hadyn said. "I should never have left like that."

She stared at him. His face looked odd; dark shadows framed his eyes in the flickering light of the fire. She didn't know what to say. He was right—it *was* all his fault. But she had never expected him to admit it.

"I lost Rusty. I had him tethered to a log and he slipped his bridle." Maggie hadn't known that she was going to say this, but as soon as she did, her eyes flooded with tears.

"Your mule?" Hadyn's voice was respectful for once, not teasing or mean.

Maggie nodded. "Maybe he'll make it home. He's smart." She wiped at her eyes.

Hadyn cleared his throat. "I really am sorry."

Maggie didn't know what to say, so she didn't say anything. Standing hunched over, she spread her father's bedroll close to the fire. She untied her flannel shirts and draped them over a bough near the fire to dry. Then she sat down.

"Take your boots off and make sure they get dry tonight," Maggie told Hadyn. He nodded and she untied her own shoes, tilting them up at the edge of the fire with a thick stone placed beneath the heels. She took off her socks and hung them on some twigs she'd shoved into the heat-softened ground close to the fire. Hadyn watched, then copied her. After a few minutes, Maggie stood up to go get more firewood. The snow was coming down even harder.

"Hadyn."

He could hear Maggie, but he didn't want to answer her.

"Hadyn?"

He rolled away from the sound of her voice. He curled up, wincing at the soreness in his muscles. For a few minutes there was blessed silence, and he drifted back toward sleep.

"Hadyn!"

This time her voice was too loud to ignore,

but still he tried. His whole body was weary. He didn't want to open his eyes. He didn't want to move. In spite of the fire, he had been cold during the night; he hadn't slept much.

"Hadyn!" Now she was shaking him gently. "Hadyn, are you all right?"

He gave up and opened his eyes. "What?"

"You have to get up. We can't stay here."

"Why not?" Hadyn sat up slowly in the bedroll. It hurt to move, and he winced again. Maggie had built a little fire. He could see the snow still falling beyond the shelter of the krummholz branches. More than anything, he wanted to lie back down, cover his face, and go back to sleep.

"I've been thinking," Maggie began. "If we head straight east, I think there's a good chance—"

"Leave me alone." Hadyn lay back down. If they were going to die in these cursed mountains, what difference did it make whether they moved on or stayed where they were? At least here they were a little warmer. He heard Maggie get up and he opened his eyes. She looked pale and weary, and she was scowling at him.

"You've caused enough trouble, Hadyn."

He shook his head angrily. "I already apologized to you. I'm sorry your father got hurt, but it wasn't my fault. I didn't want to come here. I—"

"I'm going to get back home," Maggie interrupted him. "I am not going to carry you, or stay here and freeze with you, or even spend the rest of the morning talking you into coming with me."

Hadyn stared at her as she opened her knapsack. She pulled out a flour sack and reached inside it. "I'll leave you some food, but I'm going to eat before I go." She glanced up at him as she lifted a hunk of dark red meat from the bag. She pushed the slim, sharply broken end of a pine branch into the meat and propped it over the fire.

Hadyn felt his stomach cramp and his mouth flooded with saliva. He sat up again, gasping at the sharp pain in his muscles.

Maggie was watching him. "Sore? It gets

better once you're up and moving. Here." She handed him the canteen. "The coffee is gone, but I melted some snow for water."

Hadyn drank. There was still the faint taste of coffee. The water was delicious, and once he started drinking it was hard for him to stop.

"Slow down or you're just going to get sick," Maggie cautioned. Hadyn lowered the canteen. She reached out and took it back. "I don't know what you're going to do for water, but I can't leave this. You might be able to keep the fire going and find a dish-shaped rock to melt more snow."

Hadyn stared at Maggie. "You can't just abandon me here."

She looked up. "I'll leave you the bedroll. If I can find your bag on the way down, I'll use your clothes to—"

"Wait." Hadyn felt sick. The nausea bent him forward and he struggled not to vomit. The muscles in his legs spasmed; the pain was almost more than he could stand. He let the nausea subside, then looked up. "I'll go with you."

CHAPTER ELEVEN

The smell of the roasting venison was thick in the still air as Hadyn struggled into his socks and boots. They were warm from the fire, and dry. He got to his feet, but it was impossible to straighten up all the way—the branches were too low. For a minute, he stood swaying back and forth, unable to make his cramped legs do more. Finally, he forced himself to take a single step, and then another. Bent double, he walked out from beneath the branches and stood blinking up at the dark clouds. Snow fell on his cheeks as he lifted first one foot, then the other. After a few minutes, he ducked back inside.

Maggie was right, he thought as he picked up the edge of the bedroll: His leg muscles hurt less now that he had moved around a little bit. He shook the bedding, frowning at the ache in his arms.

"Get all the dirt out," Maggie said from behind him.

Hadyn shook the quilts a little harder, then rolled them up. He set the bedroll down close to the fire. The smell of the meat was making him almost dizzy. Maggie pulled two biscuits out of the flour sack and Hadyn leaned toward her without meaning to.

"This is all I have. These and the meat."

Hadyn swallowed, holding out his hand.

"I think we should eat the meat and save these. The venison will go bad faster."

Hadyn lowered his hand. She was probably right again, but he wanted to grab the biscuits from her—both of them. It scared him, feeling like this. He had never had to go hungry in his life. He realized that he was still staring at the biscuits and raised his eyes to Maggie's face as she put them back in the flour sack. She met his eyes for an instant, then looked away, turning the meat over the fire.

Hadyn watched, his mouth watering. "When will it be ready?"

She didn't look at him. "We have to let it heat up. That way it'll warm us from inside."

Hadyn swallowed again. "How long?"

Maggie turned to face him. "You watch it. *You* tell *me* when it's ready."

Hadyn could hear the irritation in Maggie's voice. "Why are you so angry at me?" he asked.

"Because you never think, Hadyn. You make me do it all."

Before he could say anything more, she had stood up and moved away from the fire. "I'm going to fill the canteen with snow again. I'll be right back." She stepped out from under the krummholz. He could see her shoes against the snow, then she moved away.

Hadyn turned the branch over the fire. The meat was starting to sizzle on one side. He lowered it a little, then pulled it back up when it started to burn. His hunger felt like a live thing in his belly, like it had teeth of its own. Glancing back outside, he couldn't see Maggie's shoes. He reached out toward the meat. Maybe he could tear off a little strip that she wouldn't notice was missing.

Hadyn glanced back and forth from the venison to the snow just beyond the krummholz. He stopped himself, shaking his head. Maggie wouldn't have taken more than her share, and he knew it. The truth was, he would be dead now if it hadn't been for her. He turned the stick, careful not to sear the meat again. When Maggie ducked back under the branches, he looked up at her. "I think it's ready."

Maggie grinned as she set down a flat rock and placed the canteen by the fire. "If you'd said I had to wait another minute, I might have given in and said we should eat the biscuits. I'm starving." Hadyn watched Maggie pull a pocketknife from her knapsack. "Lay it on the rock," she said. "I scoured it with snow. "

Hadyn pulled the meat from the fire. It spit and sizzled as Maggie cut it into two chunks. He tried to eat slowly, but it seemed like the meat was gone all too soon.

When he looked up, Maggie was taking her last bite. She grinned again. "I feel better."

Hadyn nodded, realizing that he did too. "Thanks."

Maggie was wiping her knife, using a handful of green pine needles. She looked up. "Do you think you can walk? We'll have to cover some ground. The truth is, Hadyn, I'm as lost as you are."

"Nobody is as lost as I am, Maggie," Hadyn said. He meant it seriously, but when she laughed, he had to join in. "I've been lost since I left the road." As they talked, they gathered up their belongings and stepped out of the krummholz.

"At least the wind is gone," Maggie said, shouldering her knapsack. She handed him the bedroll.

Hadyn tucked it under his arm and nodded, glancing up the mountainside toward the rock ledges. They looked so small that he blinked.

Maggie turned and followed his gaze. "It must have snowed a couple feet overnight," she said in a low voice. Then she looked back at

him. "This isn't going to be easy." Hadyn nodded and tried to smile as Maggie led the way.

The snow was deeper than it looked. But
even worse, Hadyn's feet sank unevenly. Every
step was different. One would bottom out on
bare frozen soil about two feet down, and the
next one hit an old drift, burying his leg up to
his thigh. The layer of clean, white snow on top
gave no hint of what was beneath.

Maggie followed a zigzagging course across
the face of the slope. Hadyn soon figured out
why. It was hard enough to keep his footing like
this; headed straight downward, it would have
been impossible.

Hadyn glanced back up at the rock ledges,
only to find that they had disappeared behind
the curtain of snow. He tried to spot the
deformed krummholz thicket that had sheltered them for the night, but he couldn't.

Looking downhill, Hadyn couldn't see far
enough to spot any trees at all, but he knew
they were there. He realized suddenly that in
snowfall this thick, they could pass within thir-
ty feet of the road and never see it.

"You all right?" Maggie asked over her shoulder.

"I think so," Hadyn answered, trying to keep the fear out of his voice. She had said she was as lost as he was. He prayed it wasn't true.

A distant rumble like thunder caught Hadyn's attention. Maggie stopped suddenly and he nearly bumped into her. She was glancing around, her eyes searching the mountainside above them.

"What is it, Maggie?" She shook her head as the noise went on and on. It got no louder and Hadyn saw her relax when it finally faded. "What was that?" he asked again.

"Snowslide," she told him. "I thought for a minute it was above us. We get some big ones this time of year." She looked past him, then upslope again, squinting.

Hadyn could see how scared she was, and he followed her gaze. "How can you tell when one is about to start?"

Maggie shook her head. "You can't until it does." After one last look, Maggie turned and started off again.

Hadyn could only follow. He listened for the

dull roaring with every step. After a while, he relaxed a little. She was probably making more out of the danger than it deserved.

He walked without speaking through the ghostly landscape, sometimes falling a little ways behind Maggie, then hurrying to catch up. She didn't seem to want to talk, and he was grateful—the air still felt too thin to him and he was breathing hard.

After a long time, Hadyn noticed the first tree looming out of the falling snow. Others emerged as he and Maggie got closer. It was eerie, as though they had been standing silently nearby the whole time and were stepping forward now, revealing themselves.

"I want to go around this stand," Maggie said, stopping to face him.

"Why?" Hadyn asked. "Isn't it smarter to just go straight back down the way we came up?"

Maggie shook her head. "Don't you remember coming through there? That's the burn. Under this much new snow it would take us hours to find our way through the fallen logs and the snags."

Hadyn tryed to remember. He had been so scared that he had barely noticed anything.

"This is where I lost Rusty, more or less," Maggie said quietly. "I'll have to come back up and try to find the saddle. Papa will be furious."

"No he won't," Hadyn said. "He'll understand. He'll get you a new one."

Maggie shook her head, and he could tell that she was angry again. What had he said? He had only been trying to help out. She hitched the knapsack higher on her shoulder. "Your father might be happy to buy a new saddle, Hadyn. Mine won't be able to. Especially after the trip to the doctor in Lyons."

Hadyn looked out over the trees without responding. It was hardly his fault that her parents weren't rich, was it? After a few seconds, Maggie turned and went on. She veered to their right, away from the burned ground, heading across the mountainside.

It got harder for Hadyn to keep pace with Maggie. Somehow, she had them going uphill again. As the footing got worse, he reached out to tap her shoulder. "Shouldn't we be going down?"

Maggie answered him without turning. "If we can keep going east, we'll have the best chance—and I'm pretty sure that's east." She pointed, then pulled her hat down over her ears. "I don't think we'll have to go uphill much longer."

Hadyn hunched his shoulders against the cold. The snow muffled every sound, including Maggie's voice. The instant she stopped speaking, the silence closed in again, as if it had never been broken. If they did die up here, it would be years before anyone even found them. Hadyn blinked, trying to still his thoughts. It was stupid to scare himself.

The direction Maggie had chosen seemed to lead them endlessly upward. The icy flakes slapped at his face, and Hadyn pulled his scarf higher. He felt like he was gasping for air again. The muscles in his legs had stopped hurting, for which he was grateful. He switched the bedroll from his right side to his left. His right arm had cramped and he tried to work out the kinks as Maggie led him higher.

As the hours passed, Hadyn followed Maggie as well as he could. More than once she had to stop and wait for him. After a while he noticed she was constantly glancing up at the sky. Sometimes after she had looked upward, she readjusted their course. She was somber, serious, and he didn't try to talk to her very much.

Hadyn forced himself to keep going, even when his feet grew numb with cold again. Maggie seemed to know where she was going now. It couldn't be much farther, could it? Hadyn kept waiting for Maggie to cry out suddenly. He kept expecting her to stop and point, showing him where the road lay. But she did not turn to him; she just went on walking.

Hadyn tried to ignore the constant pain in his stomach. Breakfast seemed like a distant memory. He noticed Maggie eating mouthfuls of clean snow and imitated her, but even though his thirst lessened slightly, his hunger only got worse. He could not stop thinking about the biscuits in Maggie's knapsack. Step after step through the deep snow, he labored behind her. He started to get angry. What gave her the right to decide when they would eat?

Hadyn found himself staring at Maggie's

knapsack through the swirling snowflakes, his mouth watering. "Maggie?" She ignored him, and he said her name more loudly.

She turned. "Are you all right?"

"I'm so hungry that I feel—"

Maggie was shaking her head. "Not yet. The biscuits are for tonight." Without another word, she went on.

Hadyn reached out and caught at her coattail. "I want to eat now."

Maggie whirled around. "Do you think you'll be less hungry tonight? If you think so, I'll give you your share right now."

Hadyn grabbed the front of her coat and jerked her sideways. She staggered, thrown off balance, staring at him, her eyes frightened. Hadyn felt his anger dissolve. "Sorry."

She looked at him. "Let's just keep going."

It kept snowing all day. Hadyn walked on numb feet, his legs heavy. When the sky began to darken, he thought it was going to snow even harder. Then he realized it was evening, and he knew they would have to spend another night in the deathly cold.

CHAPTER TWELVE

When Hadyn awakened, he was huddled inside the bedroll. The low overhang of rock that had sheltered them for the night was blackened from the smoke of their fire.

Maggie had already risen. For an instant, the sight of the campfire she had built back up lifted his spirits a little. But then he remembered that they had eaten the biscuits the night before—and that now they had nothing left. He sat up, his whole body stiff and sore. Even his thoughts seemed slow. Sleep seemed to tug at him, trying to pull him back down.

Maggie was looking at him, rubbing her hands together. There were dark hollows beneath her eyes and her skin was pale. "Come get warmed up."

Hadyn nodded, but it took him a long time to make himself stand up. His shoes and socks were dry, but his feet were so cold they ached, even after he had gotten up to stand by the fire.

Maggie kept bending low, glancing out from beneath the overhang, staring at the sky. This close to sunrise it was obvious, even to Hadyn, which way was east—although the gray clouds covered the horizons, the sun was bright enough to shine through. Later, Hadyn knew, the sky would all be the same leaden gray, and it would be impossible to tell.

"Are you thirsty?"

Maggie's voice startled him. He looked up. She was holding out the canteen. He took a long drink of melted snow water, then watched as she stepped out from under the rocks to repack the canteen with clean snow.

"Are we going to freeze to death, Maggie?" Hadyn was startled by the sound of his own voice. It was thin and hoarse.

Maggie shook her head, then stopped and

shrugged. "Not if we can find the road." She stood up and pulled her coat tightly around herself, put the canteen inside her knapsack, and started off. Hadyn rolled their bedding as fast as he could, then ducked out from beneath the rock.

Hadyn lost track of time again as he walked, heavy-footed, through the ever-deepening snow. This morning, the flakes were a little larger, sticky and wet. A drip went down the back of his neck from his scarf and he shrugged his coat higher.

When the rumbling began, they were trudging along just below timberline. Hadyn was puzzled by the sound. He stopped to listen.

"Snowslide," Maggie said softly.

Hadyn glanced upslope, then stared at Maggie. "Should we run? Should we—?"

"Be quiet." Maggie held up one hand. Her already pale face had gone white.

The roar was getting louder, Hadyn was sure of it. "Maggie? What do we do? Maggie?" He was shouting now, but still she didn't turn to look at him. An instant later, she grabbed his hand and pulled him into a run.

Blindly, unable at first to hear the roar over his own panicked breathing, Hadyn sprinted beside Maggie, moving slantwise across the slope. Nearly falling in the deep snow, he managed to keep going. She turned to shout something at him and he realized that he couldn't hear her—the roaring had become too loud.

The sound of the slide encompassed everything. Hadyn fought to keep his feet, to keep going, sobbing in one ragged breath after another. Maggie let go of his hand and they separated, still running. Hadyn used every ounce of his strength to go faster, his fear erasing his weariness. He pounded over the snow, focused only on the ground ahead of himself as a roar louder than a hundred freight trains bore down on them.

The roaring swelled, shaking the ground beneath Maggie's feet, grating at her ears. She plunged sideways through a drift as high as her shoulders, then ran on, glancing sideways at Hadyn.

Suddenly, Maggie's right foot caught between

two snow-hidden rocks and she sprawled forward, barely breaking her fall with her outstretched hands. She rolled, scrambling sideways, terrified. The roaring closed in as Maggie struggled to stand, spinning in a frantic circle, unsure which way she had been going. She spotted Hadyn and began to run again, but it was too late.

The snow underfoot seemed heavy, pulling at her like deep mud. With every step, it dragged at her, moving sickeningly beneath her feet. Maggie tried to run faster, but she faltered. The slide was like an undertow, tugging her relentlessly downward. The snow rose around her like a drowning flood. She heard Hadyn screaming her name. His voice was faint against the roar, then gone.

Maggie rolled and tumbled, shoved downhill by the slide. Flailing her arms desperately, she fought to find the surface through the smothering snow; it filled her eyes and mouth, her ears. It found its way inside her clothing, grating at her skin.

Maggie managed to gasp in a deep breath,

then two, then found herself surrounded by the choking snow again. She fought for each breath, dizzied by the constant motion, bruised, terrified. The snow pressed against her. It seemed to go on forever.

Suddenly, the icy current seemed to tighten its hold on her. She struggled to make her way upward, but could not. She heard a resounding crack and felt a tremor. Then, there was only silence and darkness.

Maggie's right hand and arm were near her face. Her left arm was extended over her head. Her legs had been entrapped just as she had been struggling to make her way upward—they were extended in a swimmer's kick.

Maggie's heart beat so heavily it ached. She could not move; she could not move at all. She wrenched her body from side to side, straining every muscle against the immutable weight of the snow. Exhausted, gasping at the stale air, she went limp—and realized that she had managed to make a small space around her head and face.

Trying to calm herself, Maggie labored to enlarge her tiny air pocket. The dirty snow packed under the pressure of her right arm, giving her enough room to work her hand free. She touched her face, wiping her eyes, clearing icy grit from her mouth. As she pulled her hand away, she realized that her only hope was to somehow dig upward to fresh air.

But which way was up?

Maggie clenched her fists, feeling dizzy. She imagined taking in a clean, fresh breath and began crying. Maybe she was close to the surface, but even if she was, she had very little time.

Maggie tried to stop crying, to think. She wiped awkwardly at her eyes. Then she held very still, her whole being focused on following the tears' warm track across her cheek. Like water anywhere, her tears were flowing downward. That meant she had to dig in the opposite direction.

Hope bounding in her heart, Maggie began to wriggle around, trying to work her right hand free enough to scrape at the snow. At first she could move only two fingers, close to her face. It was so hard to breathe. Flexing her knees, she managed to lift one foot slightly, angling it as she set it back down. The sole of her shoe shaved a little snow loose. It fell beneath her foot as she lowered it.

Maybe, Maggie thought, if she could work a little more snow beneath her shoe with each try, she could gradually accumulate enough to raise herself upward—if she could somehow tunnel with her hands, too.

Maggie set to work, marching in tiny steps. With her right hand, she tried to dig at the slant she knew would take her to the surface. She had gained only a few inches when she had to stop, her breathing uneven and painful. Tears flooded her eyes again. It was impossible. She was going to suffocate.

Hadyn kept running. The roaring behind him got louder with every step. He glanced back, shouting at Maggie to keep running, amazed to see the snow boiling and swirling around her feet. Only a little ways behind him, she was trying to run across what looked like a white, rushing river. Doubled over, watching helplessly, Hadyn had time to pull in one rasping breath—then the snow beneath Maggie gave way and she was swept downhill.

Hadyn stared, turning. Maggie was screaming, fighting to stay upright. He dropped the bedroll without thinking, then ran downslope, parallel to the snowslide.

At first Hadyn could see Maggie clearly. Her face was contorted with fear, her posture rigid. Then she fell. The snow was moving deceptively fast, and Maggie was being carried along like a rag doll.

Hadyn kept running. Every time he stumbled, he scrambled to his feet, spotting Maggie almost instantly. She had sunk deeper. She was thrashing, twisting back and forth. Hadyn shouted her name as he ran, but he was pretty sure she couldn't hear him. The roar was deafening.

Toward the center of the slide, the current looked swiftest and deepest. Hadyn saw big rocks pop to the surface, then disappear again. Where Maggie was, just at the edge, the current seemed slower. There was less rock and the snow looked cleaner.

The air above the slide was fogged with white dust. As he ran, desperate to keep Maggie in sight, Hadyn passed through clouds of this pulverized ice. It stung his face and hurt his lungs. Staggering, gasping for each breath, Hadyn refused to stop.

When Maggie sank out of sight, Hadyn screamed her name, his breath quick and harsh. Then the roaring dimmed. As the slide hit the far side of the little valley, it slammed to a halt, sending up a spire of ice powder. Hadyn felt the jolt of the impact in the ground beneath his feet. Then, everything was still and everything was silent. The falling snowflakes stuck to his cheeks and eyelashes.

Startled, Hadyn realized he was no longer moving. When had he stopped running? The sound of his own footsteps surprised him as he took off again, his eyes fixed on the spot where he had last seen Maggie. He breasted a deep drift, floundering for a moment before he caught his balance.

When Hadyn reached the place where Maggie had disappeared he stopped. Bent forward, gasping in the thin air, he stared at the dirty gray snow. Here and there, tree branches and rocks jutted up at odd angles. Hadyn blinked. This was the place, he was sure of it. But exactly where should he start digging?

Hadyn stepped cautiously onto the dirty snow. It was hard, not loose. He stood, stunned. How could Maggie be alive? He scraped his boot on the gray powdered snow. Here? Or had he last seen her five feet uphill—or ten feet downhill? Hadyn's throat tightened. He would just have to trust himself.

He dropped to the ground and began digging. The snow was unbelievably hard. Looking around wildly, he spotted a stick. He ran to get it, leaving behind one glove to mark the place. Armed with the branch, he jammed his hand back into his glove and began to dig frantically.

His own sobbing breath made him stop. Hadyn sat back on his heels, despairing. It was still silent. Not even the birds were singing. He looked heavenward, letting the big flakes settle on his face. After a moment, he looked back down. A tiny scratching sound beside him made him twist around. He pressed his ear to the icy surface and heard it again.

Flinging the grayish snow in every direction, Hadyn dug madly. He jabbed the branch into the snow, loosening it, then scooped it out with both hands. He discarded his gloves after a minute or two. Throwing his weight behind the stick, he managed to enlarge the hole fairly quickly. Once it was about a foot deep, he stopped again to listen.

At first there was only silence, and his heart sank. Then the faint sound came again. As Hadyn watched, a tiny rivulet of snow fell from one side of his hole. And then another.

Laying the stick aside, Hadyn clawed at the snow with desperate fingers. Within seconds, he saw the familiar faded blue of Maggie's coat and the wide strap of her knapsack.

"Maggie!" He freed her hand and arm, digging madly, avoiding her clutching fingers. When he saw her hat, he redoubled his efforts. Seconds later, she was choking, coughing on the fresh air that streamed into the narrow tunnel he had made.

"Maggie?" Hadyn probed carefully with the stick, afraid of hurting her as he widened the opening. "Maggie?" She coughed again, but she did not answer.

Scared that the hole would collapse on her, Hadyn worked like a demon. He flung snow backward, like a dog digging out a rabbit burrow. Once the opening was four or five feet across, he started downward again. It seemed to take forever.

"Maggie!"

Her eyes fluttered open. Her cheeks were pale. For an instant he could see pure disbelief in her eyes, then she focused on his face.

"Hadyn?"

He rocked back on his heels and let out a howl of joy. He heard Maggie laugh weakly.

"I'm alive?"

It was a serious question, and Hadyn leaned down to answer her. "You are, Maggie. You are!" He touched her cheek, then put on his gloves and started digging again.

CHAPTER THIRTEEN

It was still snowing. Maggie hunched close to the fire Hadyn had built, warming her hands. Her gloves were propped up on twigs near the fire. They were steaming.

Hadyn had gone back to get the bedroll. As soon as she could stop shaking with cold, she would put on her spare trousers and both her flannel shirts. They were damp, but the clothes she'd been buried in were *wet*.

Maggie shuddered, remembering the weight of the snow, the complete darkness beneath it. She owed Hadyn her life. When he got back with the bedroll, they would have to start walking again. Maggie closed her eyes for a second, praying for strength.

When she stood up, she felt the weakness in her legs. Her stomach clenched and she realized how incredibly hungry she was. She wished for hot coffee, or better yet, the sweet apple cider her mother made with cloves on Christmas. And pie. She wanted a piece of apple pie.

Hands shaking, Maggie took out her spare clothes. She shrugged off her coat, then her wet shirt and woolen chemise. Shivering, teeth chattering, she pulled on one flannel shirt, buttoned it, then donned the other. She felt a little sick and sat down again, scooting as close to the fire as she could, spreading her hands out to warm them.

Once her violent shivering had subsided, she took off her shoes and set them next to her gloves. Then she pulled off her socks. She hung them on the stack of broken branches Hadyn had gathered for firewood. Almost immediately, they began to steam. She put her feet close to the fire, resting her heels on a thick pine branch.

Maggie looked upslope for Hadyn. She couldn't see him anywhere. With fingers clumsy and cold, she unbuttoned the flap front of her trousers. She undressed, dancing from one foot to the other. Hopping, she pulled on her spare trousers, fastening the front as quickly as she could. Then she sat down, leaning close to the fire again.

It was so cold. Maggie longed for the coziness of her family's cabin. She longed to know that her father was going to be all right. And what about Rusty? And the cattle? She shook her head, willing herself not to cry. She spread her coat across the firewood, a little mist rising from the side nearest the heat. She put her socks back on. They were still damp, but the fire had warmed them.

"Maggie?"

She stood up, startled by Hadyn's voice. "Over here!"

Hadyn came through the trees. "I found something."

Maggie couldn't help but smile at him. He was carrying the bedroll clutched against his chest. His scarf was wound tightly around his neck, covering his chin. The cold of the ground seeped through Maggie's socks. She sat back down and put her feet close to the fire. "I'm trying to dry everything out. What did you find?"

Hadyn got a rock to sit on and arranged himself on the opposite side of the fire. Then he reached into his pocket. "These. The slide must have killed them. Can we eat them?"

For a few seconds Maggie stared at the two ptarmigan hens he held, then took them from him. "These are good eating, Hadyn." She looked up at him. "I'm sorry."

Hadyn shook his head. "For what?"

"For hating you. You saved my life." Blushing, Maggie turned her head.

"You saved mine." He was silent for so long that Maggie finally looked up at him. He was staring at her. No. Not at her—at the ptarmigan. "Are we going to cook those now?"

Maggie smiled and began to pluck the small white hens. The feathers stuck to her fingers and she had to keep wiping her hands in the snow. Hadyn hovered, trying to help, mostly getting in the way. When she used her knife to gut the birds, he walked away, holding one hand over his mouth. By the time Maggie had spitted the birds and propped them up over the fire, Hadyn was back.

They kept the fire up, Hadyn bringing more deadwood when the pile was exhausted. They ate fast, one bird apiece, barely looking up between bites. The snowflakes had thinned for a while, but now came down heavily again, making a hissing sound when they hit the flames.

"Which way do you think we should go?" Hadyn was wiping his mouth with the back of one hand. He tossed the bones from his ptarmigan into the fire. The flames popped and sizzled.

Maggie didn't feel strong, but she knew she could walk—she had to. "I wish I knew," she said quietly. "Winds this time of year are usually from the east, but it's still now. I have no idea how far south we've come. Or north," she added, shaking her head.

"It has to be after noon now," Hadyn said. "I think we have to take a chance. We can't make it through another night."

Maggie forced herself to put on her shoes. Then she stood up. Hadyn had already pulled on his gloves. For a second, they stood side by side, staring down at their little fire. Maggie didn't want to leave. As dangerous as it was to stay, it seemed more risky to walk away from a warm fire into the swirling snow.

She kicked icy dirt onto the flames, wincing as the smoke roiled upward. She watched it rise straight up to the tops of the pines. Then it trailed off to one side. Maggie stared at it. "Look at that."

Hadyn followed her eyes, then narrowed his. "At what?"

"The smoke. There's a breeze up there. That could be west." She pointed in the direction the smoke was blowing.

"Which would make that east," Hadyn said, pointing the opposite way.

Maggie nodded slowly. "Maybe."

Hadyn took her hand. "Maybe is better than nothing." He gave her the knapsack and picked up the bedroll. Maggie tried to smile at him as they started off.

Hadyn followed Maggie through the trees. She was walking slowly, bent forward at the waist. He moved up beside her when they hit open ground. "I could go first for a while, break the path."

Maggie looked at him. "Thanks."

Hadyn took the lead, then looked at her over his shoulder. "You have to tell me which way to go."

Maggie pointed. "Just keep going straight. See that lightning tree on the ridge over there?"

Hadyn looked. "The big one with the top sheared off?"

Maggie nodded. "It's got a blackened side on the trunk. The smoke was in line with it, more or less."

Hadyn started walking, shaking his head. She was so smart. With his eyes fastened on the distant tree, he tried to keep up a good pace. The snow got deeper as they went downhill. At the bottom of the little valley, they had to stop and rest three or four times. Then, shouldering his way through the last of the deep drifts, Hadyn started uphill again.

As he neared the top of the next rise, Hadyn was sure they would see the road below them. He hurried past the dark-trunked tree that had been struck by lightning. He ignored his heavy legs and the aching in his lungs. At the top of the ridge, he slowed, scanning the snow-covered landscape below. There was no road, no break in the trees, nothing that distinguished this slope from any of the others they had climbed.

Hadyn swayed on his feet. Maggie came to stand beside him. He watched as she blinked, narrowing her eyes to block out some of the abrasive whiteness. Her face told him nothing, but a second later she sat down, her arms wrapped around her knees.

"Maggie, we have to keep going."

There was a long pause, then she looked up at him. "I'm not sure I can."

Hadyn stared at her. If Maggie gave up, what could he do? He had no idea which way to go.

Maggie slumped forward, and he could hear her crying quietly. Without thinking about what he was doing, he sank to the snow beside her. "I'll build a fire. You could stay here and I'll try to find help."

"You can't. You'll get lost."

Hadyn met her eyes. She was right. He would probably just walk in circles. "Get up, Maggie—we have to get going."

Maggie blinked back tears. "I'm so tired, Hadyn."

It had been snowing lightly for a while. Now the clouds opened and white curtains of big, swirling flakes fell around them. Without thinking, Hayden gripped her arm and pulled her to her feet. "You have to keep going. We can't stay here."

Maggie didn't answer. She shrugged off his hands, stepping back, then turned to face the way they had come. For a few seconds, Hadyn had no idea what she was doing, then he understood. She was sighting from where they stood now back across the valley, getting her bearings. After a moment, she began walking again. Hadyn followed closely. It was easier to keep up now—Maggie was moving very slowly.

CHAPTER FOURTEEN

Maggie shuffled along, concentrating on her footing as they started up one more slope. The pines were thick at first, then they thinned a little. She stopped to rest and felt Hadyn bump into her gently. They stood side by side. It was getting dusky.

"We have to stop and build a fire, Hadyn." Maggie's voice rasped; it hurt to talk.

He shook his head and without saying anything, started upward again. Maggie watched him, then glanced up at the sky. It had stopped snowing. When had it stopped? She shook her head and forced herself to take one step, then another.

She wasn't sure which way they were going

now. She thought they had been traveling straight east most of the afternoon, but she wasn't certain. Now, with the sun setting, the bright clouds on the western horizon were a natural compass—but had they wandered north or south? Had they walked ten miles in a straight line, or two in a circle?

Hadyn stopped. Maggie realized how far she had fallen behind. He stamped his feet in a slow, ponderous rhythm until she caught up, then he turned and went on again.

They were still pretty high, Maggie knew, but that didn't mean anything. The road home went up over three or four little passes that got up to eight or nine thousand feet. Maggie shook her head to clear her thoughts. She had been looking for landmarks all day, but nothing seemed familiar to her.

"Maggie!"

She looked up. How had she fallen so far behind again? She forced herself to hurry a little, tripping once over a half-rotted tree trunk hidden in the deep snow. Hadyn waited for her. She realized she couldn't see the expression on his face until she was close to him. It was almost dark. They walked arm in arm, holding each other up as they came over one more rise.

Maggie let herself stop, Hadyn beside her. They stood again, both swaying, clenching and unclenching their hands, fighting to keep warm.

Maggie looked out over the trees. She could barely see them. A stand of aspens mixed with pines spread out below her in an ashen mass, their trunks and branches indistinguishable in the gathering darkness.

Maggie felt the world turning, the endless sky above her head. The clouds on the eastern horizon were moving, parting like a curtain over the rising moon. Below her, the trees leapt into focus, silvered in the sudden moonlight. Just beyond the lacework of the trees, Maggie could now see a white stripe curving along the base of the mountainside.

"Is that the road?" Hadyn whispered.

Maggie tried to answer but she could only nod, grinning. Hadyn took her hand and pulled her along, breaking the way through the deepest drifts. The aspen trees were thick, but

Hadyn barely slowed down. Maggie did her best to keep up, her mind spinning with joy and relief.

Toward the bottom of the slope, the ground was rocky. Hadyn picked his way forward, sliding and stumbling, whooping once or twice when he finally stepped out onto the road. Maggie followed, smiling, her eyes brimming with tears. There were a few sets of wagon tracks slicing through the deep snow. She could also see hoof tracks. Several people had been up this way since the worst of the storm had passed.

Hadyn was stamping his feet. "Which way?"

Maggie shrugged, looking up the road. The snow looked impossibly beautiful in the moonlight. An outcropping of rock beside the road caught her eye. It was Indian Rock. Without meaning to, she cried out.

"What's wrong?" Hadyn demanded.

Maggie shook her head. "Nothing's wrong. We're close to the ranch. Closer than I thought."

Hadyn took her arm and together they began to walk again. They were still clumsy

with cold and weariness, but hope carried them
along. After a few minutes, Hadyn turned to
Maggie. "How far?"

They were rounding the last bend, and
Maggie raised one hand to gesture. "I can't see
the cabin yet, but we will in a minute."

Hadyn let go of her hand and did a shuffling
little dance, then staggered back around to face
her. "Maggie, you are amazing."

Maggie smiled. "I never thought I'd say this,
Hadyn, but you are, too." She led the way up
the road, searching the night for the amber
glow of a lantern at the cabin window. Maybe
her parents would be home. Maybe her father
would come to the door when he heard them
on the porch. He would be all right. He just
had to be.

As they turned up the ranch road, Maggie
had to admit to herself that the cabin was dark.
There were no lanterns lit. Her parents were
not there.

"Look!" Hadyn was pointing into the meadow that bordered the road.

Maggie forced herself to stop staring at the

dark-windowed cabin and followed his gesture. Rusty was standing with his long ears straight up, his head held high, looking at them. Maggie cried out. Stiff-legged, she made her way through the drifted snow and threw her arms around Rusty's neck. She buried her face in his warm fur, closing her eyes. Rusty smelled of grass and warmth and it was all she could do to make herself straighten up again.

Hadyn had his hands on his hips. "You're nicer to that mule than you ever were to me."

Maggie laughed. Pulling Rusty along by his foretop, she led him onto the road and nudged him toward the barn. With almost numb hands she lifted the drop bar and let the door swing open. She didn't have to urge Rusty to follow her now. She put him in his stall. Hadyn carried hay without being asked. Rusty lowered his head into the hayrack and did not look up again. Maggie led the way out, closing up the chicken coop on the way to the cabin. The rest of the chores would have to wait until morning.

"I'll build the fire," Hadyn said as they clumped up the porch steps.

Maggie nodded. "I'll get us something to eat." She opened the door to the cabin and went in. She pulled off her gloves, working her fingers to try to limber them up so that she could strike a match. Her breath was a plume of steam in the air. The water in her mother's washbasin was frozen solid.

The lanterns were full, their wicks trimmed as always. Maggie rubbed her hands together for a long moment, then managed to light two. Suddenly she saw a sheet of paper lying on the table. Holding her breath, she went to read it. John Cleave had made another visit.

Maggie and Hadyn,
Now you are worrying me. The mule is gone but the cows in the barn had no water. I filled their buckets and brought in the eggs, but I see no sign of a fire from last night. The hearth is cold as ice. Your father will be all right, says Billy Martin, who spoke to your mother yesterday in Lyons. With the snow, they will have to stay on a few days. I will be back tomorrow, or the following day if the storm gets worse.

With the hope that all is well,

John Cleave

Maggie waited until Hadyn had lit the fire, then handed him the note. He read it and looked up at her. Maggie crossed the room to stand before the fire. Hadyn was silent beside her as he added wood to keep the flames high and bright. They both turned back and forth, warming one side of their bodies, then the other. After a few minutes, Maggie took off her coat and Hadyn unbuttoned his. Still they were quiet.

Maggie felt tingles in her hands and feet. After a few minutes more, she took off her shoes and socks and looked at her toes. They were pink, not white—she had not gotten frostbite. She hurried to her dresser and got out two pairs of thick woolen socks.

Coming back, she handed one pair to Hadyn. "Take off your boots." He obeyed without protest and she examined his toes. "We were both lucky. Frostbite can be awful."

Hadyn was staring at her. "I'm sorry you had

to chase after me instead of taking care of the ranch."

Maggie smiled. "You can help me catch up with chores tomorrow. Besides, it looks like everything is going to be fine. Pa is going to be all right and Rusty made it home. And we're safe now." She looked at him sidelong.

Hadyn shrugged. "I just hope your parents aren't too angry with me."

Maggie grinned at him. "Are you afraid they'll send you home?"

An odd expression flickered across Hadyn's face. He frowned. "Do you think they will?"

Maggie shook her head. "No, but I thought you hated it here."

Hadyn shrugged again. "I did. But maybe the West isn't as boring as I thought it was."

Maggie laughed out loud and headed for the kitchen.